SPRING AT CHRISTMAS COTTAGE
DG Valentine

ISBN: 9798512974131

www.roswellpublishing.co.uk
IG: @RoswellPublishing

Also available from Roswell Publishing

Christmas Cottage
Winter at Christmas Cottage

Fiction
Hollyweird

Non-fiction
Send in the Congregation: Stories from the Foo Fighters Fans
Send in the Congregation 2: More Stories from the Foo Fighters Fans
Skin O' Our Teeth: Stories from Megadeth's Fans
The Human Element: PR & Marketing from a Fan's Perspective
You Are Not Broken: Tips and Tricks for Looking After Your Mental Health

For David and Stuart,
Let's visit all of the seasons together!

Chapter 1

From the stairs, Jay could see Blue sitting in the kitchen's porthole window. The big grey cat was engrossed with watching the rain, the tip of his tail twitching and his ears flicking back and forth. Blue's normal perch was in the window beside the door where, in between naps and trips to his food bowl, he waited for Dominic to return.

Jay smiled to himself at the thought of Dominic. The younger man had moved into Christmas Cottage shortly after the clock had struck midnight on a brand new year. While most of Dominic's belongings remained in the apartment above Between the Sheets, he'd managed to cram a few sets of clothes, an acoustic guitar, and the world's longest phone charger into the small cottage.

The circumstances under which they'd met had been relatively normal. In a world of online dating and apps, they'd met in Joe's Java Shack, Waybride's cosy coffee shop. Settled in front of the fire, Jay had tried his best to keep Dominic's attentions away. But the younger man had persisted and they'd ended up having an enjoyable evening doing the coffee shop's weekly quiz.

Jay had left their evening at that and gone home under the belief that he'd probably only run into Dominic very occasionally. Except that Dominic was persistent. Very, very persistent. He'd gently hounded Jay into visiting his specialist sheet music shop,

Between The Sheets. A shop that had been underfunded and on the verge of ruin. Unable to help himself, Jay had called his band's PR company and had them secretly drum up business for Dominic.

The scheme had worked and Dominic had worked twelve hour days over the Christmas period.

Jay looked forlornly at the guitar cases sitting beside the fireplace. Dominic's Christmas gift to him remained unplayed and, for that, Jay felt guilty. The guitar had been such a thoughtful gift from someone who, at the time, hadn't had a cent to spare. He could remember the earnest look on Dominic's face as though he was hopeful that Jay would pick it up and begin to play the songs that he'd packed away so many months before.

But Jay wasn't ready to go down that road yet. He wasn't ready to delve into those feelings. Dominic would have to wait a little longer to hear Winter Angels' songs played acoustically.

The feelings weren't helped by Dominic bringing his own guitar to the cottage. He played occasionally, mostly at night as snowstorms battered the small house. He'd sit on the couch and go through the songs that he knew. *Smoke on the Water. Whisky in the Jar. Go Your Own Way.* Jay enjoyed listening to him. Dominic had a gentle and calm singing voice that sounded like warm honey. It was a voice that did softened his heart and soul and made him want to spend the evening curled up next to Dominic.

Yet he still wasn't ready to pick up his own guitar.

At least not at that moment.

Leaving the instrument to gather a little more dust, Jay went to the kitchen and began preparing dinner. The day was creeping on and all too soon Dominic would be home. His larger than life personality would fill the stone cottage and his lilting voice with its Virginian accent would chase away the silence.

Blue had already moved from the kitchen window to the window beside the front door in anticipation of his friend returning home. Jay watched as the cat's tail flicked back and forth and he quietly *chittered* to the birds that he could see.

"Soon, buddy. Your friend will be home soon."

Jay smiled when Blue's ears flicked back to listen to him. His amber eyes never left the outside world.

The cottage was soon filled with the smell of cooking. Dominic was a meat and two vegetables man, although he loved any food as long as it was sweet or meaty. Salads weren't his thing and neither was anything else that could be described as "healthy".

Eventually Jay heard an excited meow. Turning from the stove, he watched as the front door opened and Dominic walked in. He dropped his bag beside the door and swept Blue up into his arms, cradling him like a baby and covering his small, furry face with kisses.

"I don't know what I'll ever do if you leave," Jay laughed. "You'll break the cat's heart."

Despite the still-cool weather and the ever present

threat of more snow, Dominic's smile was as wide and as bright as the sun. He ambled into the kitchen with the cat still in is arms and leaned in to give Jay a gentle kiss.

"We'd have to do joint custody," Dominic replied. "But from the smell of that food, I'm not going anywhere."

The laughter that fell from Jay's lips was full and deep and caused his sides to ache. Dominic's sense of humour had kept him going through the dark and often depressing months. The days where everything became too much and life seemed pointless had been few and far between with the dark-haired man around.

"I hope that there's more than my cooking keeping you here."

Dominic's eyes slowly roamed over his body and Jay felt a flush of heat touch his cheeks. "Your hot body maybe. Or your skills in the sack. Or the promise of hearing you play guitar again."

Those last words pulled at Jay's heart yet he still smiled. Putting down the spoon that he'd been using on the gravy, he stepped up and wound a hand into Dominic's long, dark hair.

"Love you, too," he murmured. "Please never leave. You complete this house."

~~~

All too soon the cottage was filled with the sounds

of people eating. Dominic, as always, was enjoying his meal. And, at Dominic's insistence, Blue got a "taste". Not that the cat hadn't already had several "tastes" while Jay had been cooking.

Dominic's decision to include Blue in everything warmed Jay's heart. They'd truly accepted one another and he often wondered if Dominic could see more of the world than he let on. Not just the physical world but the spiritual world, too. Dominic read a lot on UFOs and the paranormal and often spoke of a home out in the night sky and of how he felt comfortable just staring at the stars. His personality truly had softened in the past months and Jay was enjoying getting to know the man that he'd come to love.

There was still enough of a chill in the air to warrant having a fire. And so, once dinner was done, the three of them curled up on the couch. The fire crackled softly in the hearth and the sound was enough to lull both of them, and the cat, into a relaxed silence. With no TV to distract them, Jay read while Dominic scrolled through his phone. Blue had wedged himself between as though determined to soak up the extra heat.

Jay was slightly scared of how quickly they'd fallen into the routines of an old married couple. Every day seemed to follow the same pattern of getting up and Dominic going to work while Jay tended to the house. Occasionally he'd take the walk to Between the Sheets and potter around the shop. Sometimes he'd fetch coffee from Joe's Java Shack or tempt Dominic with lunch at one of Waybridge's many restaurants and cafes. He'd buy books from The Booknook or watch as Dominic flirted with the women that ran the local ski shops. Sometimes they'd have date nights at Stone Bridge Inn, the restaurant where they'd had their first unofficial "this isn't a date, we won dinner in the coffee house quiz" date. Everyone seemed to love Dominic and Dominic could charm his way into anyone's life.

But Jay enjoyed the routine and it was exactly what he needed after spending so much of his life living the celebrity lifestyle.

After an hour of peace and quiet that was broken only by logs popping on the fire, Dominic asked, "What are you doing tomorrow?"

Jay trapped his finger in his book to mark the place that he was at. "Going to start the garden. I've been putting it off long enough."

"Cool." Dominic's voice was filled with someone who was exhausted from the cottage's warmth. "What are you going to do to it?"

"Couple of flower beds. Vegetable patch. Gonna plant up pumpkins for fall. Bird feeder so Blue has something to watch. That awning I promised when we first met. Maybe a water feature, too."

"So you're installing a running buffer for the cat?"

Jay chuckled and placed his book on the arm of the couch. Blue stretched between them, his claws momentarily catching in the couch. "I'm sure that's not the first time that you've made that joke."

"Probably. But it's still a funny image." Dominic yawned and Jay looped an arm around his shoulder in order to pull him close. "At least it'll keep you busy."

"True," Jay replied. "Not like I've got much else to do. The cottage is pretty much as I want it. All I have to do is clean, read, and make sure that you two are fed."

Dominic shifted on his shoulder and Jay looked down to those dark brown eyes. They were filled with the weariness of the day and Dominic's happy-go-lucky personality was fast fading back into himself. "You could always pick up that guitar."

Jay felt his heart sink and he returned his attention to the small fireplace. Flames danced over the logs and raced up the chimney. "I could..."

"But you're not ready?"

"Not yet," he softly replied. "Sorry."

"'s okay," Dominic said before he broke into a yawn. "You play when you feel ready."

As the evening drew on so they retired to bed. Even that had a routine of its own, a pace that was slow and comfortable as they prepared themselves for sleep. Some nights they made love. Others they talked. Sometimes they just drifted into the warm comfort of losing themselves in a good book.

For Jay, life was finally perfect. He'd given up a fulfilling, and lucrative, career in music, a family and his old, comfortable, home in order to live his authentic self. Coming out of the closet so late in life hadn't been easy but, as he looked at Dominic, he realised that every moment of that transition had been worth it.

Dominic was propped up on a bank of pillows with black rimmed glasses on his nose and a battered paperback in front of him. The book was one of his many internet finds, an out-of-print non-fiction piece about a little known UFO crash just outside of Seattle. Jay knew what the book was about because Dominic had joyously told him. Much like himself, Dominic was fascinated by hunting out treasures in thrift stores and online.

"Going to New York in a couple of weeks," Dominic muttered.

That stilled Jay's heart. "Sorry?"

There was a rustle of pages as Dominic put the book down. "Yeah, there's a music buyers fair. I'm going to get fresh stock." The younger man grinned. "Want to come?"

"Blue?"

Dominic shrugged. "He's well behaved. I bet the hotel wouldn't mind."

Jay suddenly felt confused. His little world, the perfect little world that he'd created, was being upended.

"I don't know," he murmured.

Dominic snuggled himself down deeper into the bed. This was a sign that the other man was beginning to tire and just wanted to sleep. "Well, think about it.

The offer's there."

Was it? Or was it just an afterthought? Jay was so used to people walking out of his life once his usefulness had worn out that he wasn't surprised by Dominic's sudden announcement. In fact, he was was kind of surprised that Dominic had hung around for as long as he had.

Jay's issues were life long and had required decades of therapy. They'd also manifested in the drinking problem that had put him into rehab. His Mom had died young and, following her death, his Dad hadn't been overly present. They'd made their peace in the time before his father passed, but Jay had continued to live with the scars and search for a place that he could feel comfortable. Sometimes the band's fans were his family. Sometimes it was the family that he'd built for himself. Sometimes family had been his band. Now his family was Dominic and Blue and Jay was terrified of losing one part of that little unit.

Jay sighed and reached for the light before mentally scolding himself. Of course Dominic would need to travel and get new stock. Between the Sheets wasn't like his old barbecue business where everything was delivered to the door. Most of the music that Dominic sold was probably rare and from people's attics. The sellers may be old school and unwilling to sell online. Plus there was the added bonus, at least for Dominic, of being able to get a large amount of stock in one place rather than picking and choosing single items from the internet. Dominic needed to go to those sellers. He'd be back at some point.

"Blue'll miss you," Jay quietly said.

"I know." There was a smile in Dominic's voice. "But I'll call every day."

Chapter 2

Jay woke the next day to Dominic snoring softly beside him and Blue purring in his face. Dominic was not a morning person. Blue definitely was.

Slipping from the bed, Jay shoved his feet into a pair of snug slippers and let the cat dash for the stairs. Paws softly landed on the exposed wood of the steps and Jay quickly followed before Blue started his noisy morning protest.

Dominic's words from the night before still rattled around his head. Jay was used to being alone and had been for a good while before Dominic had shown up. He was also used to people walking out of his life. People walked in wanting something and left once they had it, often with little to no time to form any kind of bond. He himself was guilty and had often chased one night stands, both male and female, in order to try and find that connection.

But he couldn't escape the feelings that he had for Dominic. Feelings of love, safety, security, and peace. Dominic had wormed his way in and Jay had fallen hopelessly in love with him. The hollowness that had followed him for so many years had finally disappeared.

An annoyed meow tore through the kitchen and Jay shook himself from the wasteland of memories that he'd been occupying. Reaching into a cupboard, he pulled out two pouches of cat food.

"What do you want this morning?" He peered at

the pouches. "Chicken? Or shrimp?"

As with every morning, Jay leaned down and held the food out to Blue. The cat appeared to consider both before brushing up the pouch of shrimp.

"Good choice. Chicken will just sit heavy at this time of the day."

Jay made of fuss of feeding Blue. He washed out the water bowl and filled it with cool, clean water. He did the same with the food bowl, making sure to get rid of any crumbs of the previous day's meals. Once the dish was dry, he set about tearing open the pouch and forking the chunks into the bowl. Finally he set everything down in front of his impatient cat and watched as Blue went to work.

"Spoiled," he softly chuckled. "You're so spoiled."

Blue did little more than flick an ear.

And, as if on cue, the stairs began to creak as Dominic slowly made his way down. As always, he was wrapped in a blanket and his hair was held back from his face with his glasses. He yawned, his eyes still closed as he felt his way to the kitchen. And so began the ritual of feeding the second hungry person.

Once Dominic had gone to work, Jay grabbed a pen and a pad and sat himself at the table. He drew a rough outline of the garden and began to work out what was going to go where. The top corner, with its overhanging pine trees, would be the perfect place for a bench and water feature. The bottom right corner, with its abundance of sunlight, would be great for growing vegetables.

It was early March and there was still snow on the ground. There was still the threat of more snow until at least April. But Jay had already decided to clear what snow there was into water butts to use at a later date. He was determined to make the garden as self-sufficient as possible.

Blue had stationed himself at the opposite end of the table. His eyes watched the pen scratch at the paper while his tail twitched across the polished surface. Jay eventually had what he decided was a decent plan of action. The next job, and the one that he was dreading the most, was actually clearing the garden. Sure, he could hire in someone to do it for him. That would be pocket change to him. But there would be no pleasure in watching someone else create his perfect space.

Changing into clothes that were more suitable to working outside, Jay grabbed a shovel and began to move the slowly melting snow into the three large butts that stood down one side of the cottage. The work was slow and, to him, backbreaking. It had been a long time since Jay had lifted anything heavier than the cat or the groceries and, before long, he was leaning on the shovel and sweating in the gentle late-winter sun. Sweat beaded his forehead and his breathing was laboured.

Jay glanced around himself and groaned. Only a small portion of the garden had been cleared. The snow that had drifted up beneath the trees was still there as was the layer that tangled around the weeds.

All he'd really managed to do was clear the space that was already paved.

"Shit," he murmured. "Maybe I am gonna need help?" Jay sighed and looked at the sky. "Or maybe you can rain and wash this away for me? No? Okay, I'll carry on."

After several minutes of rest, he went back to work. Taking the wheelbarrow around the garden, he loaded it with snow before wheeling it to the water butts and unloading. Rinse and repeat. He'd only done half of the garden before twinging muscles began to scream. With a limp in his step, Jay returned inside and prayed that there would be no more snow.

He lay on the floor in front of the fire with one arm tossed over his eyes. The occasional groan whispered past his lips and Blue was purring up a storm beside him. Jay had read somewhere that a cat's purr vibrated at the right frequency to help heal wounds and ease aching muscles. He didn't know if it was just an old wives tale but he was happy for Blue's presence.

"I don't smell dinn- Holy shit, are you okay?"

The door slammed in Dominic's wake and footsteps hurriedly echoed on the wooden floor.

"Nothing." Jay moved to pull himself upright and groaned as his back throbbed. Sighing, he lay back down. "Okay. I was clearing the garden and pulled a couple of muscles. That's all."

Dominic knelt beside him. His face was filled with concern. "Doesn't look like just a couple of muscles.

22

Want me to help you?"

Jay didn't want to admit defeat but he feared that he had no other option. A hand was placed in the small of his back, easing him into a seating position. Pain bolted through him and Jay resisted the urge to howl. Stars burst behind his eyes and his head pounded as his back twitched and spasmed.

"Should be okay in the morning," he muttered through gritted teeth.

"Doesn't look like it will be. Come on. I'm gonna get you in a hot shower and make sure we can get you comfortable. Do you have heat packs or anything like that?"

Jay nodded and waved a hand in the general direction of the kitchen. Years of head-banging had left him with easily pulled muscles, while years of hauling a guitar around had, at some point, helped to even it all out a little. But it had been a while since he'd done any kind of weight training other than pinning Dominic to the bed and it showed. He hurt all over and injuries that had long been forgotten were beginning to rear their ugly heads again.

The one thing that Jay dreaded to think about was his addictions returning. He'd often drank to numb the pain. Not just the pain that darkened his soul but also the physical pain that tore at his body. He'd been in his forties before he'd had to concede and tell himself that he wasn't getting any younger. Lying on the floor of his home, aching and trying not to cry, had been some of the worst moments of his life. Physical therapy had helped and he'd tried to steer clear of painkillers through a fear of becoming addicted to those, too. Rehab for alcohol had been hard. Rehab for painkillers would be even worse.

He allowed Dominic to help him to the shower. Stripped of his clothes, Jay sat with his back against the cool tiles and allowed the hot water to cascade over him. He shivered although, for the moment, not through pain. The water soothed his aching limbs and the sound spoke to his soul. There was a connection to water and its movement that he'd acknowledged many years before. He enjoyed being beside the sea, the lakes, and the rivers of the world. When it rained, he enjoyed nothing more than to listen to the sound. The feeling of water against his skin seemed to be one of the highest pleasures alongside having the one he loved beside him.

Jay had a feeling that he'd be spending a lot of time in the shower the second Dominic left the house to go to New York. That ache was still present, gnawing at his soul and reminding him that Dominic would soon be gone. Old fears of abandonment were beginning to raise their heads and Jay was fighting to keep them down. He didn't want to find himself begging Dominic to stay. Dominic had given him the option to go but, to his old wounds, that still felt like an afterthought, a moment when Dominic had remembered that he'd be leaving and had forgotten to tell Jay.

"Got you some warm pyjamas." Dominic's gentle

voice broke the sound of the shower. Through the steamed up glass, he could see the ghost of the younger man nervously shifting from one foot to the other. "And, yeah, I know this sounds odd but I can try and rub some of those pains out for you." Dominic shrugged and tucked the pile of clothes under one arm as he shifted his hair back behind his ear. "Used to do it for the guys that worked for me. A day of hauling wood and shit around plays havoc with your body."

Jay knew that he couldn't push Dominic away. Just because the dark-haired man was doing something without first consulting him was no reason to punish him. Jay needed to have a long chat with himself and remember that Dominic had a life and job that had come long before they were together. For them to be able to work as one, Jay needed to let go of the fears and issues that had clung to him for so long. Yet they were fears and issues that had been with him his whole life and which he'd spent years in therapy and, ultimately, rehab for. He just needed to remind himself of all that he'd learned and not try to control Dominic or their relationship. If he did, Dominic would be gone and the world that they'd built together would shatter.

Leaning his head against the glass, Jay managed a soft smile. "I'd love that. Thanks."

"You stay there a minute and I'll get everything ready. I'll come get you." And, with that, Dominic was gone. From the shower, Jay could hear him opening and closing drawers and pulling things from the laundry cupboard.

Letting his shoulders fall back against the slick tiles, Jay turned his face into the spray. Everything was beginning to feel better. He knew that he'd overdone shovelling snow the first time that he'd stopped. But determination had won him over and, stupidly, he'd kept going to the detriment of his ageing body.

Jay could feel his worries washing down the drain. Worries of Dominic and himself, worries about Dominic going to New York, worries that Dominic would never come back. All of them were slowly disappearing as Jay gave himself the mental talking to that he needed. Not reacting negatively to what was happening would serve them both well in the long run. But he knew that he needed to talk more to Dominic about his life and how what seemed like sudden spur of the moment decisions made him feel.

"You ready?"

Opening his eyes, Jay peered through the steam to find Dominic standing beside the door. The ghostly figure moved back and forth until Jay wearily pulled himself to his feet and stepped from the shower. Dominic was waiting with a pile of fresh towels in his arms and a small smile on his lips.

"Get dried off and come into my therapy room." Dominic shrugged and his smile widened to the one that Jay knew, and loved, so well. "Well, the bedroom."

Jay did as he was asked, water dripping to the tiled floor as he wrapped towels around himself. Getting to the bedroom was easy and a simple step forward found him looking at blankets and pillows spread across the floor. Floral scented candles flickered on one of the bedside tables and Dominic had perched himself on the edge of the bed.

He nodded to the floor. "Face down and put your arms on either side of the pillows."

In that moment Jay knew better than to question Dominic. With his back and shoulders still protesting, Jay eased himself back to the floor. Thick thighs straddled his hips once he was stretched out and strong hands rested at his shoulders.

"Relax," Dominic murmured. "At least as much as you can."

Jay muttered a sarcastic reply which only the pillow heard before closing his eyes. Dominic began to knead at his tender flesh, his fingers working into the muscles and finding the newly formed knots. The pain from each pass felt as though his skull was splitting open and Jay did his best not to buck Dominic from his back. He hissed and groaned and balled his hands into the warm blankets.

Yet, as Dominic moved lower and began to focus on his spine and ribs, Jay found himself relaxing. His eyes became heavy and he melted into the comfortable nest that Dominic had created for him. The soft smells of the scented candles floated around him and Jay could imagine himself to be anywhere but in the cottage.

"You know," he mumbled slowly, "we should go travelling. You ever been to Europe?"

"No, sir," Dominic quietly replied.

Jay took a deep breath and turned his head to one side. With his eyes cracked open he could see beneath the bed. He tried to ignore the odd sock, discarded books, and dust bunnies.

"I'll take you to some of my favourite places." Jay smiled as the memories began to flood in. "There's so many restaurants that you'll love. Where do you like to visit?"

Dominic's hands paused at his waist and Jay could feel the other man breathing as he mulled over the question.

"Didn't used to see much when I was on the road with the barbecue." Dominic began to move his hands along Jay's spine. "We'd set up in whichever field or parking lot we were in and sleep in our RV. If we were lucky, we'd have a hotel to stay in. But, most of the time, because there was food already cooking or marinating, we stayed close to where we were serving. We only saw the towns and cities as we drove in and out. But if I had to pick somewhere, maybe London. Paris, too." Dominic paused as he worked his thumbs in above Jay's hips. "Heck, I think I'd love to see all of Europe."

Lifting his head, Jay yawned. "We'll do it, then."

"That would be great." Dominic's thumbs dug a little deeper causing Jay to hiss. "How you feelin'?"

"Better," he softly replied. "You're really good at this."

A gentle kiss was laid between his shoulders. "Thank you. I try. Want to get a little more comfy?"

Easing himself from beneath Dominic's healing hands, Jay took the soft, warm pyjamas that Dominic had retrieved from the bathroom. Slowly he dressed himself before looking to Dominic. The younger man had his hands clasped before him and a gentle look on his face. Reaching out, Jay tucked some of Dominic's hair behind his ears and leaned in to give him a kiss.

"Thank you. I appreciated that."

"You're welcome. Go and make yourself comfortable on the couch. I'm gonna call the Mexican place and get some food delivered."

Jay happily sank into the welcoming curves of the couch. With his head against one arm, he swung his legs up to dangle over the other. Blue, happy to see him again, hopped up to lie on his chest. After a moment of turning around and making biscuits, the big grey cat settled down and closed his eyes.

A few minutes later and Dominic's hands lifted his legs. The younger man sat himself down before resting Jay's ankles in his lap.

"Food is on its way," he said. "Should be here in about thirty minutes."

Everything was perfect and felt like a scene from a movie. He had his man and his cat. A fire roared up the chimney and its warmth embraced them like an old lover. Little lamps chased away the rest of the darkness and, other than the fire, the only other sound was Blue purring.

They fell into a peaceful silence with both of them watching the dancing flames of the fire. The time didn't always need to be filled with talking or activity. Sometimes just sitting and enjoying the other's company was enough to fulfil their needs. For Jay, it was a bit of a relief. When he'd first met Dominic, the younger man had a habit of being over-exuberant and excitable. As time passed, he learned that Dominic's true personality was hidden behind the child-like wonder. He could be quiet and calm and gentle. He could settle and do nothing for an hour or two. The personality that the wider world saw was just for show, the man who was used to putting on a show whether he was cooking or selling music. He was a people pleaser through and through and Jay was grateful that Dominic had been able to settle enough to show him his other, calmer, side.

Eventually there was a knock at the door and Dominic quietly excused himself. Quiet whispers reached Jay's ear and there was the distinct sound of cash being exchanged. As the door closed so the smell of rich, Mexican food began to tickle his nose. Blue dived off his chest and chased Dominic into the kitchen. For once, Jay was going to allow himself to be waited on. Shifting to a sitting position, he could hear Dominic preparing whatever was in the bags and Blue harassing him for treats. Jay didn't even need to look to know that Blue would be standing on his hind legs with his front claws hooked into Dominic's jeans.

Paws pounded against the floor and Blue hurled himself back onto the couch as Dominic ambled in with two plates piled high with food. Jay smiled and took one from the younger man.

"Thank you for this. I appreciate it."

Dominic broke into his patented million watt smile. "You're welcome. Cat's got your cutlery."

A frown furrowed his brow and, resting the plate on his knees, Jay turned to look at Blue. The grey cat stared back at him and, ever so slowly, closed his eyes. Tucked beneath his collar were two rolled napkins. Jay plucked one out and slid the knife and fork out.

"You're silly," he said with a smile.

"And you love it! Bonne appétit."

There was something about sitting on the couch and watching nothing but the fire as they ate. Peaceful, homely, and what he'd always wanted. Nothing needed to be said except for the happy sighs of people filling their stomachs. In fact, eating seemed to be one of the things that they enjoyed doing together. When they weren't eating, Jay seemed to find himself gravitating towards the kitchen or heading to the supermarket. One of the reasons he wanted to grow his own vegetables was so that they could have more variety.

He was just picking at the Peruvian chicken when he felt something snag a thread in his jeans. Looking down, he found Blue resting a paw against his leg. There was an almost expectant look on the cat's face.

"If only you could talk," he murmured. "Not that you need to. I know exactly what you're saying."

Stripping off the spicy layer, Jay offered out slivers of juicy chicken. Blue knew better than to try and take his hand off. Instead, sharp teeth delicately pulled the meat from his fingertips before the cat devoured them. Only once he'd finished those did he try the same trick with Dominic. And, as always, the younger man gave in, too.

Chapter 3

"I've got to go and pack," Dominic murmured between mouthfuls. "I leave on Monday."

Jay felt his heart plummet and the pangs of loneliness return. "I know."

Between the Sheets had become incredibly successful and, according to Dominic, was exceeding his wildest dreams. He'd expected the shop to turn over enough profit for him to live off and enjoy life. Instead, Dominic had found himself at the centre of a perfect storm and was doing everything that he could to keep everything going.

And Jay knew that would sometimes mean letting Dominic go. Glancing down at his empty plate, Jay quietly continued, "We need to talk."

"Have I told you how much I hate those four words?"

He smiled and peered up at Dominic. "Several times."

Dominic leaned back into the couch and whispered, "You need to talk. I can feel it."

"I do." Placing the plate on the floor, Jay pulled his legs up onto the couch and faced the younger man. There was concern on Dominic's face and the younger man was reaching to play with his moustache, a bad habit that Jay only saw him do when he was nervous. He reached out and placed a hand on Dominic's knee. "Don't be concerned. This is about me, not you. Dominic, I have a lot going on. You know that. You know about my family and how I've spent so long fending for myself. That's left me with a lot of issues. Some you know about. Some you don't yet. But you will. One day something will happen that will trigger another issue that I realise I need to talk to you about."

Jay sighed and continued to gently stroke Dominic's knee. "I have abandonment issues. Pretty big ones, as I'm sure you can imagine. I get attached to people and then hurt when they walk out of my life. This happens *a lot* in the music industry. You think you're making a connection with someone and, suddenly, a week later you're old news and they're attached to the next person. It's fuckin' painful for someone like me. So when you said you were going to New York, my mind instantly went into overdrive and I honestly thought that it was an excuse for you to leave."

"Which is why you threw yourself into shovelling snow?" Dominic softly interjected.

He gave Dominic a crooked smile. "Exactly. I'm not saying that you have to, but a little more notice of you going on buying trips would be great. Just a little reassurance that you're not packing and leaving."

"I could never leave you." In the light of the fire, Dominic's eyes were wide and glazed. He looked to be on the verge of tears and Jay welcomed him with open arms when he shifted closer. "I wouldn't leave you. Jay, you're everything to me. I hope that you know that. Warts an' all. We all have those warts. We all have issues. We'll help one another to heal. How does that sound?"

He leaned in and pressed a kiss to Dominic's head. "Sounds wonderful. And you've already done so much for me. Thank you."

With his head tucked beneath Jay's chin, Dominic snuggled down. "Same."

Tangled together on the couch, they enjoyed one another's presence. Jay felt no need to move, not even when Blue climbed over them in order to wedge himself against the couch. Instead, he gently stroked Dominic's back and listened to his gentle breathing.

Maybe he had done more than he thought possible for Dominic. He'd definitely noticed the younger man slowing down as he'd settled into life at the cottage. There had been less time scrolling through his phone and more time doing the things that mattered like building a relationship and a home to be in. Maybe Dominic had been searching for something, too, and had found it within the walls of Christmas Cottage?

Gentle kisses traced his jaw and hands slid beneath his shoulders. The smile never left Jay's face as he held Dominic close. He could feel the younger man's heart beating and Dominic's warm breath against his cheek.

"Love you," Dominic whispered.

His heart, previously in shreds, now soared with the love that he felt. "Love you, too."

There were another few moments of silence before Dominic quietly continued, "Want to go to bed?"

Those were the words that Jay had been waiting to

hear. "I'd love to."

~~~

He woke the next morning to aches that hadn't been there the previous night. The pain from gardening had faded to nothing. Instead, his thighs were deliciously sore and Jay smiled at the memory. Dominic had done what Dominic always did when he needed attention; he'd stripped naked and started talking dirty. It had taken very little for Jay to get involved and the early hours had crept around before either of them had fallen asleep. He made a mental note to try and catch a nap before Dominic got home.

As he was descending the stairs, Jay also remembered that it was Saturday. In two short days, Dominic would be on a plane for New York. The days since Dominic's announcement that he was going away had passed so quickly. Far faster than Jay had ever thought they could.

But Dominic would be coming home and Jay was determined not to get into the dark place that had seen him run to therapy so many times before.

"You're gonna be okay," he muttered to himself as he started the coffee machine. "Don't sweat it and don't harass him while he's away. It's the last fuckin' thing either of you need. Just let him go and do his thing and come home."

Water began to gurgle through the machine and Jay set a pan on the stove to make oatmeal. There was a pained meow as he was fishing around for the ingredients and he found himself switching to pulling out tins of cat food.

Blue sat at Jay's feet with his large amber eyes firmly trained on his food bowl. It didn't take more than a couple of minutes for Jay to get it from pouch to bowl to floor but, in that time, he was convinced that the cat thought he was going to die from hunger. He'd seen the same response from Dominic. Both cat and partner seemed to need feeding on a three hour schedule and it was a process that Jay had found kept him on his toes.

"Maybe that's what I'm gonna miss?" he said to the cat. "I'll only have you and me to feed for a few days. Life's going to be a little easier and I'm going to have a little more time."

"Talking to yourself or the cat, Hammond?"

A blush raced up Jay's cheeks and he looked up to find Dominic standing on the stairs with a soft smile on his lips.

"Don't stop." Dominic walked down to him and took Jay's face in his hands. "Don't ever stop being so sweet and so caring. I love hearing you talking to Blue. And I know that you're worried about me coming back. But I'm gonna come back." The younger man leaned in close enough for their lips to touch. "Always gonna come back to you. And why wouldn't I? You're everything that I've ever wanted and more."

Jay felt himself stall. His heart plummeted and his doubts begin to rise. "But-"

"But nothing." Dominic gave him a gentle kiss, his fingers wandering to knot in Jay's waves of silver hair. "I don't want to hear about how you think I'll leave because you're not skinny, or young, or look like you did twenty years ago. I'm in love with you, here and now. I'm in love with this guy. The guy who wears his heart on his sleeve and his scars on his skin. I don't know if I'd want younger you. But I want this you. I want the you with the paunch and the wavy, silver hair and the arms full of tattoos. You grew from that shy kid who was too afraid to speak into this man who gives his all and encourages everyone else to be the person that they are. I want everything that you are, baby, and I won't hear a word against you."

His knees were weak and Jay could feel himself stepping off the verge and hauling Dominic back to bed. Instead, he wrapped the dark-haired man in his arms and held him close. He ran his hands along Dominic's spine and up into his hair as they kissed. He felt the younger man purr against his chest as they fell a little deeper in love.

"Go to work," he mumbled. "Before I drag you back to bed."

Dominic chuckled and pulled away. There was an impish grin pulling at his lips and dancing through his dark eyes. Jay had seen it many times before and it was a sign that Dominic was seriously debating staying home and getting naked. That had happened once shortly after New Year. Dominic had decided he'd needed another day off and they'd spent the entire day in bed. Not that Jay had complained as it had been the perfect way to chase away the winter cold.

For once, the younger man ate his breakfast and wandered out of the house without so much as another perverted word falling from his lips. There were, however, muttered threats about returning for "lunch" and "getting a quick one in before New York."

The words should have made Jay feel like a piece of prime meat. Instead, he was on top of the world. Dominic didn't show his love in the same way that others had, which gave Jay enough reason to think that Dominic wasn't entirely of this Earth and was still trying to learn about human interactions. The thought always made him smile and, reassured that Dominic loved him as much as he loved Dominic, he returned to the garden.

Being careful not to overdo himself, Jay cleared the rest of the snow and began to hack away at the weeds. The sky was a beautiful, clear blue and the first warm rays of spring sun touched his cheeks. The sweat returned to his brow but Jay didn't care. He was enjoying creating a space for them to relax in. A part of him was suddenly a little sad that Dominic wouldn't be away longer. The thought of him returning to a space that was ready for them to take over warmed him in a way that he hadn't felt for a long time.

With his back beginning to twinge, Jay took a break

and grabbed a coffee. He sat at the table and scrolled through his phone in a hunt for a machine that would yank the weeds from the ground and save his ageing back. A local rental company had just what he was looking for and Jay put a down payment on both that and a machine to turn over the impacted soil.

Christmas Cottage had been empty for several years before he'd bought it and the lack of love to the garden had showed. He'd stood at the back door and looked at the overgrown wasteland with despair. The thought of hiring people to trek around his house and do the garden over had made the idea of being alone almost unpalatable. Jay had chosen the cottage for just that reason; the chance to escape everyone. Except that hadn't lasted long either and now he had a cat and a partner vying for attention. Not that he minded. He adored both Blue and Dominic to the ends of the Earth and would give up neither. It was the idea of strangers that made him feel cold.

Once his coffee cup was empty and Blue was full of snacks, Jay headed back outside. With a little pain now flaring in his lower back, he was cautious not to do anything to exacerbate the issue. Instead, he cleared away the debris from his earlier hacking session. There was already a container ready and waiting to be used as a composter so Jay dumped everything in there.

With his arms folded across his chest, Jay stepped back and took a look at the plot of land before him. Where there had once been a tangle of weeds there was now a nearly empty garden. For the first time he could see the soil and it allowed Jay to better visualise what he wanted to do. He decided that, while Dominic was away, he'd start hunting around the local garden stores to see what he could find. Specifically the bench that he wanted to go beneath the trees. Maybe some chimes to hang in the branches for when the wind whispered through the leaves.

A shiver ran along Jay's spine and he smiled to himself. In his mind's eye, he could see the garden. He could see Dominic and himself sitting on the bench while a summer rainstorm rolled through the sky. He could hear the raindrops on the leaves and smell the dewy scent of a world enjoying life.

"Lookin' good!"

Dominic's voice startled him and Jay swung around to find the younger man leaning against the door frame. His hands were stuffed in his pockets and his long hair was pulled back into a ponytail. A bright smile lit his face.

"You've done a good job." Dominic nodded to the garden. "You can actually see the ground." He stepped out of the door and walked up to Jay. "Not lookin' bad yourself either, Hammond."

Jay felt his breath hitch as Dominic placed a hand on his chest and looked him straight in the eye. The smile narrowed to a smirk.

"Said I was coming back for lunch," the younger man purred.

Shaking his head, Jay reached out and touched his

fingers to the other man's chin. "You're something else, aren't you?"

Dominic's smirk deepened and his eyes shimmered with the lust that Jay had seen so many times before. "You're only just working this out? Besides, seeing you out here with sweat glistening on your skin is driving me crazy. There's no way that I can wait until tonight."

He leaned in and gave Dominic the barest of kisses, something to whet his appetite, before pulling away. "Come on, then. Let's get you fed and on your way."

Within fifteen minutes Dominic was back out of the door and Jay was staring at the ceiling with a feeling of serenity swimming through him. He laughed and shook his head as he thought over the absurdity of Dominic closing up his shop and racing home for a quick bout of sex before dashing back out again. In fact, he shouldn't have been laughing because, in the world of Dominic, that was a perfectly normal occurrence. He was surprised that Dominic hadn't done it more, although he suspected that "lunch" back at the Cottage would now become more of a regular event. Making a mental note to prepare himself for the invasion of horny Dominic at lunchtimes, Jay slid from the bed and got himself dressed.

He found Blue sitting beside the bed with his head cocked to one side as he watched Jay. Looking at the cat, Jay shrugged. "What? It's not like you've never seen us do that before."

Going downstairs, he gathered up an armful of vegetables and sat himself at the table. The cottage was quiet and Jay relished the moments of peace. He loved Dominic. He also loved time to himself.

Dinner was going to be one of Dominic's favourites; stew and potatoes. With the cooler weather still hanging in the air, the younger man appeared to enjoy bowls of vegetables and meat covered in a thick gravy. All of it to be mopped up with home-baked bread.

Jay peeled and chopped vegetables while watching the sun through the lounge windows. It danced through the still-bare branches and tickled the now-thawed driveway. Layers of defiant snow still clung to the trees, hidden in the shadows and away from the rays of the sun. In a few hours, Dominic's tiny car would pull onto the driveway and the cottage would, once more, be filled with love and laughter.

Chapter 4

Monday dawned all too soon and it was with a heavy heart that Jay helped Dominic to load one full suitcase and several empty ones into the trunk of his car. He felt emotional as they stood on the doorstep, the younger man's arms around his neck as he was fed passion-filled kisses. Dominic promised to call every night and, by the tone of his voice, Jay suspected that the dark-haired man would have only one thing on his mind whenever he picked up his phone.

"Travel safe," he murmured. Burying his nose in Dominic's hair, he inhaled the other man's scent. "Call me when you land."

"I will. I promise. Love you." Dominic's voice was soft and gentle and Jay was broken at the thought of being parted from the man who'd so easily filled the cracks of his life.

"Love you, too. So very much."

Dominic gave him another squeeze before taking a step back. Despite the smile, he looked sad as though he'd hoped that Jay would change his mind and go along with him. "Go and work on the garden. It'll take your mind off me not being here. And, admit it, you're gonna enjoy the peace and quiet for a few days."

The tears were already beginning to prickle his eyes. He was determined not to cry in front of Dominic, nor to show him just how much the separation was affecting him. "I will."

Dominic gave him another tight smile before getting in his car. Standing on the doorstep, Jay watched as Dominic backed out and hit the road, the younger man waving as he headed away from the town and to Denver airport.

By Dominic's own admission, it was the first time he'd left Waybridge since he'd set the shop up. He'd arrived laden down with stock and had managed to keep everything ticking over thanks to finding new items online. But with the rush that Christmas and all the positive publicity had bought him, he needed to do a proper restock. And that meant leaving town for a while. There was no use buying piecemeal from the internet when he could buy in bulk and for lower prices.

Jay stepped into the road and watched as the little car disappeared over the hill and into the distance. Co-dependency had never really been one of his issues. He'd lived, quite happily, with his wife for many years while having clandestine relationships on the side. Once those relationships finished, Jay would shrug and move onto the next one. There were two distinct sides to him. The one that hooked up with people for sex and very rarely mourned when that ended (mostly because he'd been so drunk he'd forgotten come morning) and the other side that did mourn when a connection he believed was flourishing suddenly withered and died.

With Dominic he had everything that he hadn't had in other relationships. In his marriage he'd had a companion but not someone he'd consider a lover even though she'd carried his children. In his one night stands he'd had lovers but now anyone he'd consider a partner. Dominic was both; lover and partner. And that combination was throwing up the terrifying prospect that maybe he was becoming dependent on Dominic and his presence. Again, it was something that he would have to work through and talk to Dominic about.

Going back into the cottage, Jay found Blue perched on the back of the couch. The big, grey cat was screaming his head off, a sign that Jay had forgotten to feed him.

"Five minutes, Blue. I'm five minutes late. Seriously, between you and Dominic I'm not sure who's more of a handful when their dinner is late."

He didn't give the cat chance to jump down. Instead, Jay swept him into his arms and hugged him close. Blue may have believed that he was dying a slow, painful death through starvation but he still allowed himself to be hugged and kissed.

Jay carried him into the kitchen and carefully placed him on the floor. Blue then began his dinner dance around his bowls until Jay had everything that he needed on the counter.

Once Blue was fed, Jay returned to the garden. The machines that he'd ordered had arrived and Dominic's departure was the perfect excuse to put them to good use.

The weed puller fired up with a guttural gas-powered roar. Pushing it onto the freshly shorn ground, Jay felt it go to work. He watched with a delighted satisfaction as the remains of the weeds landed in the hopper.

Two trips to the compost bin later and the ground was cleared. All that remained was the clean slate of bare soil. Standing at the edge, Jay surveyed it with the joy of a job well done. And he'd barely broken a sweat which he chalked up as a good thing. Sweating lead to pulled muscles and there was no-one to rub them with Dominic out of town.

He was just about to fetch the rotavator when a movement among the trees caught his eye. Being a hunter, Jay was well accustomed to the fleeting glimpses of animals among the flora and fauna. But there was something different about what he was seeing. For a brief moment, he thought that maybe Dominic had returned and that the whole trip to New York had been a hoax in order to play some elaborate prank.

Whatever was among the trees twitched and Jay felt his blood run cold. He could take on intruders but it was the fear that he was being *watched*. So far, his life in Waybridge had been peaceful. No-one bothered him and only the kids at the grocery store really questioned him about his life. Those he didn't mind. The kids were sweet and gave him a wide berth when they weren't in work, leaving him to live his life quietly.

No, it was the fear that one of the band's many

rabid fans had finally tracked him down and was about to make his life very, very difficult. Finding him wouldn't have been hard, not after their official social media accounts had posted so much about Dominic's shop. Jay had just hoped for another few months of solitude before they all came tramping up the driveway. Or for them not to bother at all. Waybridge was so remote that anyone who'd wanted to stalk him would have to sink a lot of time, effort, and money into reaching him.

The shadows moved once more and Jay could hear feet shuffling through snow and long-fallen leaves. He held his breath as he waited, his fight or flight mode well and truly engaged. The cottage door was only a few feet behind him and he knew that he'd be safely indoors before whoever was in the forest reached him.

The fear that gripped his soul suddenly gave way to relief as a deer ambled from the trees and into the garden. Standing in the shadows of the bare branches, the creature stared at him before taking several tentative steps towards him. The shadows beyond it moved and soon a small herd of deer were standing in his garden, their dark, long-lashed eyes focused on him.

Jay couldn't help but smile. There was something joyful about seeing them. He'd occasionally seen herds crossing the road between patches of forest. He'd even considered renewing his hunting license. Again, that had been something that he hadn't gotten around to.

They all stared at one another and, unsure of exactly what to do with a herd of inquisitive deer, Jay made his way back inside.

Only for him them to follow him to the door. His smile widened and the joy that he felt was beyond measure. But there was something distinctly unsettling about them following him around. Feeling something brush against his ankles, he looked down to find Blue wriggling between his feet to investigate the new arrivals.

"Yeah, you've never seen deer before." Reaching down, he picked the cat up and cradled him close. The last thing he wanted was for the deer to spook and crash into his house. "These are deer. You've eaten some in the past."

Jay winced at the words. Things from his previous life were starting to feel a little unsavoury and uncomfortable. Staring into their large eyes, Jay had the feeling of the sentience that lived within them. There was more life in the deer than he'd ever acknowledged. But that had been because he'd mostly seen them through the scope of his gun.

The cat and the deer sniffed at one another. Each of the larger animals took a turn at inspecting Blue. When Blue stretched out to rub his head against one of them, Jay knew that the deal was done. The deer were friends.

"Bet they're coming into town looking for food. Let's see what we can find them."

Hoisting Blue onto his shoulders, Jay raided the fridge for every fruit and vegetable that Dominic had promised, and failed, to eat. He was just chopping them into chunks when he heard the unmistakable sound of hooves on tile.

"No, no, no, no! Not in here!"

Swinging around, he came face to face with one the deer. Its large dark eyes firmly focused on him and staring straight into the depths of his soul. He'd never met deer so brave, nor so brazen, before. His only experience with them had been while he'd been hunting. Hours had been spent hiding from the creatures as he'd tracked them through forests only for them to end up on his dinner table.

Yet there appeared to be intelligence and understanding in the animal's eyes. Jay felt himself still as they looked at one another, lost in a trance as he tried to comprehend what he was seeing. The animal's large, furry ears flicked back and forth as it listened to its new surroundings.

Slowly he reached for a piece of apple and placed it on the palm of his outstretched hand. It lasted for less than a second before the deer scarfed it down and the others began to barge into the kitchen in search of their own snacks.

Patience was not the herd's virtue, much like Blue and Dominic, and Jay did his best to wrangle the pile of fresh produce outside. A good chunk went missing in the several seconds that it took him to get to the door, snaffled down by over eager and over friendly wildlife.

There was something strangely comforting about feeding the deer. Their muzzles were fuzzy against his hand and they were far gentler when taking food than he thought they would be. Jay found himself softening towards them. Maybe he'd underestimated the creatures that roamed the same forests that he did. For so long he'd been a part of the community that believed in helping to keep numbers at safe levels. They could, as he well knew, become a nuisance if there were too many of them. But standing in his newly weeded garden with a group of deer carefully taking food from his hands was putting them into a new light.

~~~

The fire had burned down and the cottage was cosy and warm. Propped up on pillows and with the bed's blankets tucked around him, Jay flicked through the book that he was reading. He'd found himself lost in a series set in London and had already spent many happy hours sourcing them from various thrift stores.

He was just getting warm and comfortable when his phone rang. Plucking it from the folds of the bed, he answered it to find a sleepy Dominic smiling at him.

"Hey, gorgeous." Dominic's voice was slow and tired. "Look at you all tucked up in bed. Shame there's no-one to keep you warm tonight."

Jay grinned and placed his book to one side. "Hey! Thanks for calling."

Dominic chuckled and appeared to push himself down into the bed. The wall above the bedhead was some kind of muted gold and Jay could see the lower part of a silver photo frame. "I'm trying to butter you up. Make you feel good. And that's all that you have to say?"

Jay's smile widened and he could feel a blush on his cheeks. The bedside lamp threw warm pools of light onto the grey stone walls and Blue was purring up a storm beside him.

"Sorry," he softly replied. "You caught me at a good part of my book."

"Can let you go back to it. Although I'd prefer to stare at you for a while."

Jay honestly didn't think that he'd stopped smiling since Dominic had first walked into his life. Dominic was a constant source of light and joy, a happy-go-lucky personality to compliment his own quieter one.

"How was your day?" Dominic asked.

Jay yawned and let himself slide deeper into the bed. "The garden's weeded and ready for planting. I also had visitors."

"Anyone I know?" There was a mischievous twinkle in Dominic's eyes as though he was thinking that Jay may have been having fun without him.

A soft smile tugged at his lips. "Don't be getting ideas. The deer are obviously hungry. They came into the garden and then followed me into the cottage. So I gave them all the healthy stuff that you'd promised to eat."

Dominic sighed and, for a moment, averted his eyes from the screen. "Sorry. I'll eat them next time."

"It's okay," he softly said. "Someone enjoyed them."

The image on the screen wobbled as Dominic moved. He'd pushed himself up against the headboard and Jay had the perfect view of his face. "Interesting because I've been having deer visitors. Food must be scarce this year."

"Must be." Jay paused and frowned. "Wait? They visit the shop?"

Dominic nodded. "Yeah. Didn't have anything the first time so I gave them some pastries. Now all they want is pastries and not the oats that I bought."

Shaking his head, Jay laughed. "You're something else."

Dominic stretched, yawned, and used his free hand to scratch the back of his head. "If I remember rightly, that's a compliment."

They talked back and forth before sleep began to take over. It had taken Jay a long time to admit that he wasn't eighteen any more and that late nights caused some kind of hangover the following morning. After an hour of talking to Dominic and showing him Blue, Jay shut off his phone and placed it on the beside table. The cat had curled up on Dominic's side of the bed and seemed smug in having so much space to himself.

Smiling, Jay gave Blue's head a scratch. "Enjoying all the space? Or sad that your friend isn't here?"

Blue just purred and stretched his head into Jay's hand. The house was unusually quiet without Dominic gently snoring beside him. Dominic had filled so many of the dark cracks that his absence had been almost instantly evident. The moment that his car had pulled off the driveway had been the moment that Jay had been unsure of how he'd lived without another in the house. The cottage had needed another soul adding to it before it fully became a home. But it couldn't have been any old soul. It had needed to be the right one. And despite their occasional differences, Dominic seemed to be the person who added that little extra spark.

Rolling onto his side, Jay buried his nose into Dominic's pillows and inhaled the other man's scent. A sprinkling of dark hairs covered the crisp white pillows and there were still rumples from where he had slept the previous night.

Jay knew that the time apart would do them good. And it was something that he had to keep telling himself. He couldn't cling to Dominic as he had done in previous relationships because clipping the other man's already-stretched wings would doom what they had.

Turning out the light, Jay stretched across the bed and settled down. They may only have been together for a handful of months but the presence beside him had been calm and welcoming. Its absence was duly noted. However, the extra space was a blessing and Jay fell asleep with a smile on his face.

Chapter 5

"Are you for fucking real?"

Leaning his hip against the kitchen counter, Jay stared at the back door. Four furry faces stared back at him, their ears pricked forward as they watched and waited to see if any snacks would be forthcoming. Blue was standing on his back legs with his front paws against the glass and meowing at his new friends.

Jay grabbed his phone and snapped a quick photograph of the inquisitive deer. He sent it to Dominic with the added note, *Yours do this?*

He knew that Dominic was out and busy with his shopping so Jay placed the phone to one side. Trying to ignore his audience, Jay went about making breakfast and coffee. With Dominic not at home, he would normally have eaten while leaning up against the kitchen counter. But he couldn't do it. Not with so many eyes trained on his back.

The dusty smell of the previous night's fire hung in the air and the only sound was the clock ticking in the kitchen. Even Blue had calmed down after chattering to the deer for several minutes. Everything was peaceful and just as it had been several months earlier.

Jay could remember those early days before Dominic had formally moved into the cottage. He remembered how still the building had been and how sometimes the only sound would have been the fire crackling, or his feet on the stairs, or Blue quietly snoring on the couch. There had been a brief moment when there hadn't been any entertainment in the cottage; he hadn't even accessed videos from his phone. At some point in the time between Christmas and March, a small radio had appeared in the kitchen. It picked up several local radio stations although he'd found that the digital aspect wasn't so good. But the small faux-wood device was good for picking up news and weather warnings.

Jay had been adamant in his desire to not have a TV in the cottage. Dominic had questioned him a handful of times before settling down and appearing to enjoy the more quaint way of life. For Jay, watching TV was like staring into the void. It bought all that was bad into his living space and it was the negativity that he was seeking to escape from. As well as that, his personality, as addictive as it could be, would latch onto certain shows and issues and keep going through them until he wore himself out. And it was that exhaustion that he found to be an issue. The tiredness behind the eyes and the constant ache of the brain made him cranky and irritable. Eventually he would spiral into a place where he disconnected from family and friends. So in order to be present for those in his new life Jay had decided to keep all but books and music from his life.

Eventually Blue dashed across the table and roused Jay from his thoughts. Sighing, he got to his feet and took his dirty dishes through to the tiny kitchen.

The deer were still loitering outside. There

appeared to be no way to disperse them other than to give them some kind of nutritional offering. Digging the dry oatmeal from the cupboard, Jay opened the door and tossed a few handfuls out. The deer scattered in search of their treats and, with a sigh of relief, he closed the door and leaned against it.

Getting out was the aim of the day. He needed to go to the garden supply store. Jay still hadn't renewed his driver's license so his primary mode of transport was his own two feet. They store would deliver although normally Jay would get Dominic to cram as much as he could into his little run around car.

With Dominic on his mind, Jay picked up his phone. There was no reply to his earlier text and the gnawing that Jay thought that he'd dealt with began to grip his stomach. *What if?* That's what was rolling through his mind. What if Dominic wasn't on a buying trip? What if he'd met someone else and couldn't break it to Jay? What if he'd decided he needed a break but couldn't talk about it? So many questions and no answers.

"Come on, Hammond. Get yourself together. You've been to therapy for this. You've worked it out. Dominic's not gonna leave you. He said so himself. You looked into his eyes as he said it. He's staying put."

Pushing himself deeper into the cottage, Jay forced himself to get ready to go out into the crisp March morning. He put on jeans, a sweater, and a jacket before slipping his feet into well worn boots. Finally, he put Blue into his harness and hoisted the cat onto his shoulders. The sound of the cat purring in his ear was soothing and Jay felt himself smile as he headed for the door.

The walk would do him good, he knew that. And it was the perfect day for walking with clear blue skies and the barest hint of cool in the breeze. Thawing mud clung to the soles of his boots and the sky could still be spotted among the branches. Buds had started to appear in January and their shoots were already tickling his legs as he walked through the trees and down to Main Street.

Pickens Garden Supplies was at the top end of Main Street just a short hike behind Joe's Java Shack. The cobbled streets had long been cleared of snow and there were only a handful of ski-suited tourists milling around with take-out coffees. Stores were readying themselves for the new season with changing displays and new products. Jay paused before a couple of windows in order to examine what was inside. Blue stretched himself forward as though doing the same and Jay felt himself smile.

It felt good to smile. It felt good to be out of the house. It felt good to be breathing the air. Yet, as he looked at his reflection with his shoulder length grey hair and grandfatherly paunch, he began to question exactly why Dominic wanted to be with him. Dominic was younger, albeit not by many years, but still retained far more of his youthfulness.

"No," he quietly murmured to himself. "Not going

down this route."

Shaking his head, Jay pulled himself away from the tourist store's frontage and continued his walk up the gently sloping street. On his left, the mountains, still capped in snow, soared away in a haze of blue. The air was as clear as it could be and Jay enjoyed drawing it into his lungs. The lengthening days and warming air felt like a rebirth and he could feel his mood lightening as he neared the top of the hill.

He passed Between the Sheets and smiled softly. A sign, that read "Gone shopping. Back in a week", was tacked to the door.

Slipping down a narrow alley beside the coffee shop, Jay found himself standing in an open parking lot. The highway roared by a few hundred yards away. Beyond the sweeping strip of asphalt was the gently sloping foothills of more mountains.

To his left and to the top of the parking lot was a small strip mall comprising of a big box supermarket, an auto repair shop, and Pickens.

Dodging through the traffic and with Blue still clinging to his shoulders, Jay crossed the parking lot and made his way into the store.

Pickens smelled of compost and untreated wood. They were smells that bought back so many memories for Jay. Memories of working at his old house. Of putting together sheds and extended the house. Of the hard work that had turned it from a shell and into a home. But he didn't have time to stand and dwell on the past. He wandered beside piles of bagged compost and past racks of early blooming plants in the foyer.

People milled around with their elbows resting on the handles of flatbed cars. They wandered from one section to another, inspecting purchases before making a decision.

Jay grabbed a cart and scooped Blue from his shoulder. He set the cat in the little fold-down seat that was normally reserved for children and looped the leash around the cart's handle. Blue stared up at him and gave Jay a slow blink.

Smiling, his scratched his cat's head. "Spoiled. You know that, right? Both you and Dominic. Spoiled."

He began wheeling the cart around the large, open plan store with some idea of what he was looking for. Flowerbeds, or something to make them from. A bench. A small water feature. Plants. Vegetables. A bird feeder and accompanying feed.

Like the other patrons Jay wandered at a leisurely pace. A few people stared at Blue but most were lost in their own worlds. For Jay, it was a break from normal life and the routine that he and Dominic had built for themselves. He was enjoying just looking, picking up ideas, and browsing all that the store had. Picking up items, Jay turned them over in his hands before returning them to the shelves or placing them on the cart.

It was a little late to be planting flower seeds but Jay found all that he needed for the vegetable patch. The seed stands covered a good portion of the store's floor space and Jay stood in a patch of bright sunlight as he examined countless packets and boxes. The sunlight flooded the white-tiled floor and warmed the back of his neck. A sense of peace and happiness settled over him and, for a while, Jay allowed himself to just *be*. There was no pressure to get home and do *things*. He could, for a while, just *breathe*.

Vegetables could be planted in the spring and harvested in autumn. There were plenty on his cart, ready to be checked out, including pumpkins. The multitude of brightly coloured packets had caught Jay's attention and he couldn't help but pick up more than he needed. But they would keep for the following season. And, if he was lucky, he could harvest seeds from what he'd already grown and use those. The garden was the project that he needed to keep himself busy and away from the thoughts and doubts that continued to plague him.

The sweet smell of wood was tantalising to Jay and he continued to wander through the sprawling store and towards the outdoor area. Out the back were racks of trees, bedding plants, water features, and ready-built planters. He wandered among the displays of wood, noting down product names and numbers. As he did, Jay found himself stopping beside a long, narrow trough. Yes, it was a planter but if the garden was going to have wildlife, then they needed feeding. And that included the deer.

By the time that they left Pickens, his stomach was rumbling and the sun was beginning its descent towards the horizon. Jay had left everything that had been on the cart with the delivery desk, put the seeds in his rucksack, and paid. At some point that week, everything would arrive at the cottage and he could spend a happy few afternoons putting it all together.

Blue was grumbling on his shoulder which meant that there was only one thing to do; find food.

There were numerous restaurants and cafes to choose from but Jay forever found himself drawn back to the same one. Stepping into the Java Shack, Jay let the warmth and welcoming smells wrap around him. He'd tried to keep his tradition of stopping by on quiz nights but that had fallen by the wayside as he'd settled into a routine with Dominic. He debated picking it up again once Dominic was back home. An evening out would be a nice change to being in the house.

He ordered a coffee and a meat platter. As always the coffee shop was busy and the only available seating was beside the fire.

"Okay with the cat?" he asked.

The young barista smiled at him. "As always, Mr Hammond, it's a pleasure to see Blue."

At the sound of his name, Blue's ears shot forward and he gave a pitiful meow. That obviously tugged at the blonde woman's heart strings and she reached beneath the counter for a box of treats.

"Gentle," Jay quietly instructed. "I know you're hungry."

Jay was impressed by how delicately Blue removed the crunchy treat from the barista's fingers. He then settled back on Jay's shoulder and savoured it. Reaching up, Jay scratched the cat's head.

"Good boy," he murmured.

"We'll bring your food over when it's ready," the young woman said. "Why don't you go and take a seat. Get rid of some of that chill."

Jay gave her a warm smile before heading to the fire. Flames crackled up the blackened chimney and the armchair was as comfortable as Jay could remember it being. Once settled, he plucked Blue from his shoulder and settled the cat beside him. His hand idly stroked the animal's thick fur as he watched the fire.

There were so many memories attached to the tiny part of the coffee shop. Meeting Dominic. Reluctantly taking part in the quiz. Talking until the fire burned low. And what Jay had considered a hollow promise to visit Dominic's shop.

Oh, how the tables had turned.

He smiled as he settled back into the chair. With one leg crossed over the other, he allowed himself to drift into the warm and happy thoughts that danced through his mind. In those early days, Dominic had been skittish and excitable. He'd been a joy to be around. And, as he'd made his way into Jay's life, that joy had only grown. Dominic made him laugh every day of the week and loved him harder than anyone else ever had. He was perfect and Jay was sorry that he'd been doubting the younger man. Letting him go in order to go and shop for his business had been hard and Jay knew that he needed to be readily accepting in that part of Dominic's life. Yes, Dominic could quit and live a life of luxury on Jay's dime but it was obvious that he didn't want to. He wanted to be productive and put some good out into the world. And, in all fairness, it would be cruel of Jay to contain and keep Dominic's lovable personality to himself. The world needed Dominic, just like Dominic needed them.

The wooden board of meat, bread, and salad arrived and Jay grabbed Blue's harness before the cat could dive onto it. In hindsight, his treatment of Blue had lead to the cat having a larger than life personality which, on occasion, meant having to deal with him acting as though harassing people for food was okay. If he admitted it to himself, Jay loved Blue just the way he was and wouldn't change the vocal cat for the world.

And so he hand fed Blue slivers of beef, chicken, and turkey before tucking in himself. He purposefully left the venison. Suddenly that didn't appeal to his appetite.

The scene was perfect except for one little detail; Dominic wasn't there to enjoy it with them. There were no appreciative moans or comments about the food. No talking everything and nothing over coffee. No just sitting back and enjoying the warmth of the fire. And Jay realised that his phone had been surprisingly quiet all day.

Taking his phone from his pocket, Jay turned on the

camera and positioned Blue and himself so that the setting was obvious. He snapped a quick picture and sent it to Dominic.

The only thing missing from this is you. Speak to you soon.

The message disappeared into the ether and Jay buried the phone into his rucksack. With a full stomach and a purring cat, Jay settled back to enjoy the fire.

~~~

He still had to lay a fire when he got home. Despite the slowly rising temperatures, the cottage was still cold. The sun wasn't yet up long enough to warm the thick stone walls. Jay knelt before the fireplace with a bucket beside him and swept the ashes out. A pile of fresh logs sat beside him and he'd refilled the log basket before he'd allowed himself to take his coat off.

His phone started to ring just as he was setting the logs in place. Leaning back on his heels, Jay reached to the couch and picked up the device. Dominic's name scrolled across the screen and, with a smile, he swiped to answer.

"Hey. Wondered where you'd got to."

"Been shopping all day." Dominic sounded tired but happy. "You know this fair is over several venues, right? And none of them are even remotely close to any of the others. Started out at Madison Square Gardens today, which is the biggest of them, and finished up at the Sheraton over in Brooklyn."

With his phone trapped against his shoulder, Jay shifted himself to sit. "I didn't realise this was so big. And I certainly didn't realise that it was held in so many different places."

"Yeah. Most of 'em are hotels and the hub is obviously at Madison. But still." Dominic yawned and Jay could hear the sounds of New York in the background. Cabs, horns, sirens, and people talking made something twinge deep in his soul. He wanted to be back out on the road and seeing places. Exploring and taking photographs before coming home with a handful of too-good-to-be-true stories. "I'm heading back to the hotel. Can I call you when I've had a shower and something to eat?"

Jay smiled softly. "Of course you can. I'll speak to you later."

"Love you. Speak soon."

And before he could reply, Dominic was gone. Jay sat with his phone in his hands for a few moments before looking back to the still unlit fire. He shrugged.

"Better get this finished or we'll freeze tonight, cat."

Chapter 6

Once the fire was roaring up the chimney and the warmth was beginning to chase away the cold, Jay went to the kitchen to start dinner. If truth be told, he'd forgotten how to cook for one person and was sorely tempted to just call for take out. Mexican seemed appealing, as did steak from the restaurant that they loved. Instead, he tossed a few handfuls of vegetables and some stock into a pan and set them to boil.

"Maybe tomorrow," he muttered to himself. "Take out tomorrow as a treat."

He was just about to put the peelings into the bin when the strange sensation of being watched rippled over his body. The cold tingle ran up his spine and landed in his shoulders. Looking up, he found a handful of deer clustered around the kitchen's tiny windows.

"Oh no."

He could have thrown the trash from the vegetables away but that felt like a waste. Opening the back door, Jay gently shooed the deer back a few feet before scattering the remains of the potatoes and carrots on the ground.

"Sorry it's not a lot. I've got better stuff coming, I promise."

Only he hadn't. The trough was on order but the farm supply store was at the opposite end of Waybridge. Taking his phone from his pocket, Jay set a reminder to call the store and have deer feed delivered. They could still eat, even if it was from the ground.

As he watched the deer, Jay felt a sense of peace settle over him. There was no desire to get his gun, nor to kill the creatures before him. Instead he marvelled at how docile they appeared, accustomed to the presence of humans from their days hanging around the outskirts of Waybridge. He knew that the deer population needed to be kept under control. But he also knew that it wouldn't be him doing the hunting.

A young fawn, probably only several months old and already well-used to seeing humans, bleated and trotted up to him. The normally shy creature shoved her head into his hands in the ultimate show of trust. Jay smiled and gently cupped her delicate face. Large, dark eyes stared up at him and he felt his heart melt as he ran his fingers over her fuzzy face and furry ears. Jay spoke softly to her as he enjoyed the connection. He'd never found himself so close to a deer before, at least not while they were alive. His heart was full of love and joy as the fawn pressed herself closer.

Once they'd eaten, the deer, including the fawn, wandered back to the trees. Jay couldn't help but stand and watch them. They were graceful and far more beautiful than he'd given them credit for. And, to their credit, they were giving him a change of heart.

~~~

Dinner was finished and the sun had long since set before his phone rang. Sitting on the couch with only the fire and a table lamp for light, Jay dumbly looked at the vibrating device in his hand before realising that it was ringing. Quickly he swiped to answer before Dominic once more disappeared into the darkness.

"Hey!"

"Hey! Sorry!" Dominic was lying in bed with his dark hair spread over the white pillows and his phone held above him. "I took a shower, ate a really great burger, and then fell asleep. It's been a long day."

Smiling, Jay settled down into the couch. Blue shifted beside him and rested his head on Jay's knee. "I gathered."

"Yeah." Dominic yawned and appeared to stretch. "Got a lot of new stock but I still need more. Tomorrow's the last day and pickings are starting to get thin so I'm going to head up to Boston. There's a new fair that's only just popped up on the radar." Dominic yawned again, seemingly oblivious to the dark cavity that had just opened up in Jay's soul. "I should be another week and then I'll be back. I promise."

"Okay." It was the only word that Jay could think of and Dominic picked up on the sudden quietness.

"You okay?" the younger man softly asked.

Jay wanted to answer in the affirmative. He wanted

Dominic to be happy and to explore his new and abundant life. But he also felt the younger man was dishonouring his wishes to keep him informed of his movements.

Yet Jay realised that he couldn't force himself onto Dominic. He couldn't let his own issues control the both of them. Dominic deserved all the happiness in the world. A year previously, the dark-haired man had been goodness knows where. Probably selling up his barbecuing business before moving to Waybridge. At the same time, Jay would have been settling himself and Blue into Christmas Cottage and trying to build a new life for himself.

"Yeah," he finally sighed. "I'm okay. Just these old insecurities that's all. I've got to beat them, Dominic, and not let them rule us. You know I'm scared that you'll leave us and find someone, or something, better. But I have to trust that you're going to come home."

"I know." Dominic's voice was soothing and gentle and Jay could feel it lulling him into a sense of security. "I would have told you earlier but even I've only just found out. I just need to get another case of stock and I'll be set. Hopefully for the year."

"How often do these fairs happen?"

Dominic attempted to shrug against a bed that appeared to be extremely comfortable. "Every six months. Winter and summer normally. Like I said, you'll have to come with me next time. We'll take a trip between a couple of 'em and you can show me all your favourite sights."

Dominic's smile was as soft as his voice and Jay found himself responding in kind. He trusted Dominic and, deep down, he knew that they younger man would return.

"That would be nice. I'd enjoy that." Jay sighed and turned his attention towards the fire.

There was a pause and Jay closed his eyes. The warmth of the fire rolled over him and he curled his toes into the rug.

"You're sounding good tonight," Dominic whispered.

"Yeah?"

Jay recognised the change in Dominic's tone and a smile tugged at his lips.

"Yeah. Don't think I'm not watching you. You're sprawled on that couch and enjoying the fire. The warmth is doing you good. I can see the colour in those cheeks."

His smile widened and he cracked an eye open. Dominic was smiling at him from the tiny phone screen. His free hand was wound in his dark hair and his eyes were already heavy.

"Something you want, Dominic?"

"Oh, always," the younger man purred. Dominic shifted in the bed and he arched his neck before settling back down.

His attention was now fully back on Dominic. "And what would that be?"

"You. Always you."

"Want me to talk dirty to you?" Jay softly asked.

"In that voice? Yes fuckin' please!"

With his legs stretched out before him and a bulge growing in his own jeans, Jay detailed exactly what he wanted to do to Dominic upon the other's return. No sordid stone was left unturned and no debauched detail was left uncovered as Jay allowed Dominic to disappear down the rabbit hole of his fantasy. Jay watched as, across the country, Dominic slid his hand from his hair and down to his groin. His soft moans and gentle groans were music to his ears and only prompted him to become more lewd.

"Show me," he purred. "Show me what will be all mine when you get home."

For the next twenty minutes, Jay watched as his partner pleasured himself. Soft sighs and moans drifted across the airwaves as Jay continued to talk. He spoke of all the things that he wanted to do. Some of them quick, some of them so slow that Dominic would pass out from the pleasure. He wanted naked skin, and shimmering sweat, and nights of sex in front of the fire before it became too warm to do so. From across the miles, Dominic gave a strangled moan. Jay felt the need to make excuses in order to relieve himself.

"You," Dominic whispered. "Want to see you get off."

Heat raced to Jay's cheeks and he glanced to the dying fire in the hope that was the source of the sudden warmth. "Me?"

"Yeah." Dominic opened his eyes and gave Jay a slow smile. "Go an' put your phone on the mantelpiece and let me see you jerk off."

"I-Dominic, I'm not sure."

"Why not?" Dominic's smile was the happy, loved up one that Jay adored so much. "Wouldn't be the first time I've seen you enjoy yourself."

There was a lump forming in his throat and Jay did his best to choke it back down. "Is the connection secure? I." Jay paused and took a deep breath. "I don't want anything getting out there, you know?"

Dominic gave him his patented lopsided smile. "That's completely understandable. I just wanna watch you when I get home. I wanna lie in bed and watch you have the time of your life while I tell you exactly what I want to do to you."

The blush on his cheeks only deepened and Jay found himself smiling. Dominic had referred to the Cottage, and himself, as *home*. A place where he felt safe, loved, and secure.

"It's a date," he said. "On your first night back."

"Awesome! Thank you." Dominic paused and settled back into the bed with a yawn. "Love you."

"Love you, too, Dominic. Probably more than you'll ever know."

"Nah." The younger man stretched and knotted his hand back into his hair. "I know. I can feel it. Feels good."

Jay went to bed happy and filled with love. His confidence in Dominic's return came and went but their fireside chat had left him with the knowledge that his partner would, eventually, come home. That homecoming may be a few weeks into the future and Jay had to keep reminding himself that his loneliness wasn't forever. That, too, would fade and be little more than a distant memory.

Learning to embrace being by himself had been hard. For so long he'd searched for his perfect family and, over and again, he'd deluded himself into believing that he had it. Only for that knot of people to eventually disappear from his life.

At first, the loneliness had been a dark hole in his soul. The pain had been beyond measure and Jay had sought comfort in alcohol and the arms of one night stands. Waybridge had been the place for him to really rebuild himself and, in the few months prior to meeting Dominic, Jay had found himself becoming comfortable with the single life.

Jay relieved his pent up tension in the shower before settling into bed with Blue. The cat had taken up residence on Dominic's side of the bed and appeared to be enjoying the extra space. And, in truth, Jay enjoyed the company of his feline friend. Blue had been with him since before his divorce. He'd always had cats and dogs although that number had dwindled in the later years of his marriage until just Blue was left. The large, grey, very friendly cat was more than happy to pack his own little bags and set out on a new adventure.

From his vantage point in bed, Jay could see over

the wooden bannister and down into the main living area. The chandelier hung from the wooden beams with silk threads of spider web laced around its arms. A portion of the dining table was also in his line of sight. And, in the far corner beside the window, was the black guitar case. A thin layer of dust had settled over the top.

Jay felt his heart ache as he looked at the guitar. He really did need to pick it up even if it was just to hold the instrument in his hands.

Blue gave Jay a confused look as he slipped from the bed and crept back downstairs. He quietly crossed the area and silently stood before the black guitar case. His breath had caught in his throat and Jay rubbed his itching palms against the soft fabric of his pyjama bottoms. There was a nervous excitement in the air; it had been a handful of years since he'd last picked up a guitar and the thought of doing so once more both excited and sickened him.

But it was like riding a bike, right? You never forgot how to play a guitar. At least that was Jay's hope.

Wrapping a hand around the handle, Jay heaved the case away from the wall and up onto the table. His fingers brushed over the cool silver latches before hooking beneath them. They gave a satisfying click as they snapped open and Jay felt his anticipation rise.

The hinges sighed when he lifted the lid as though they'd been waiting for Jay to brave opening the case. Nestled within the velvet lining was the light-coloured guitar that Dominic had so gleefully handed over on Christmas Day. The pick was still trapped between the strings and Jay felt a twinge of nostalgia as he reached out to touch the shaped plastic.

With his breath caught in his throat, he wrapped a hand around the neck of the guitar and lifted it free. A thick black strap uncoiled from behind the guitar and Jay felt a strange sense of contentment as he swung it over his shoulder.

Settling the guitar around himself was as natural as breathing. The weight and shape felt safe and loving as though an old friend had wandered back into his life. Wandering around the living area, Jay plucked at the strings and savoured as the thin metal bit into his soft fingers. He'd have to build up callouses again if he wanted to go back to playing. But, for the moment, he was content in listening to the soft sounds that each one made.

The instrument in his hands was a portal to another dimension, a place where Jay could express his innermost feelings without a worry or care. He mostly avoided reviews of the band's albums and continued to create whatever came to mind. Feeling the warm wood against his palms and the strings against his fingertips was akin to returning to a home that he'd all but forgotten about. A home that had, for a long time, been a distant memory stored at the back of his brain.

Jay sat on the couch and stared into the dying embers of the fire. The ashes rustled as they settled. Quietly, and in the midst of the darkness, he began to pluck at the guitar. Chords that he thought he'd long forgotten began to flow and the silent room was soon filled with the sound of familiar songs.

Hearing those songs and feeling the guitar resting on his knee was a balm to Jay's soul. Tears stung his eyes and he took a breather in order to wipe them away. He hadn't realised how much he'd missed playing until that moment. Being a musician had died the day he'd walked away from his previous life. He'd packed those memories into boxes and slung them into a storage unit before making a vague promise that he'd return one day. In reality, he'd never intended to pick up a guitar again.

But playing and creating was who he was. It was in his blood and etched into his genes. Walking away may have been easy at the time. But returning was even easier and Jay settled back onto the couch to run through the catalogue of music that he'd spent so many decades writing.

Chapter 7

Jay woke to find himself on the couch with the guitar on the floor beside him. His body ached and, true to life, Blue was standing on his chest and shrieking like a hell-fired banshee. There was also another sound, one that Jay hadn't expected to hear.

Grabbing the cat, Jay righted himself with a grunt and forced himself to his feet. Arranging himself as best he could, Jay dived for the door and found a twenty-something man in a Pickens uniform standing on the doorstep with his arm bent and ready to knock again.

"Morning, Mr Hammond." The man grinned. His name tag read *Phil*. "Got your order for you right here. Where do you want it?"

With a wriggling Blue clasped to his chest, Jay leaned out of the door and pointed to the gate to the left of the house. "Gate's unlocked. Can you put it down there, please? I'll move it into the garden."

"Can put it in the garden for you."

Jay smiled sleepily. "Just there is great. Thanks for the offer though."

Phil gave a small nod and his smile widened. "No worries. Cute cat."

"Thank you."

While his purchases were being unloaded, Jay quickly fed a protesting Blue and dug around in his wallet for some cash. He pulled out a twenty dollar bill and went around the side of the cottage to find

Phil.

The delivery man was stacking pallets against the wall and smiled when Jay appeared. "Nice place you've got here. It's great to see someone taking care of Christmas Cottage."

Looking up at the rough stonework Jay nodded. "It is a lovely little place."

"The last owners loved it, too. They just outgrew it eventually and moved across town. Shame that it sat empty for so long. I always thought that these storybook houses were in high demand. But, hey, I'm just a guy shifting wood for a living. What do I know?!"

Jay chuckled and held the cash out. "Thanks for you help, Phil. Really appreciate it."

"Any time." The young man smiled. "And thanks. Appreciate this."

They bid farewell and Jay watched as the truck pulled off of the small drive before heading back into the house. Blue had already scarfed his breakfast and was sunning himself in the kitchen window. Taking a bowl from the cupboard, Jay made himself a serving of oatmeal and went to inspect his haul.

The plastic wrapped pallets sat against the wall with their labels facing outwards. He'd bought a handful of flowerbeds and, of course, a trough for his hungry deer. Jay knew that the deer were going to be a problem and had decided to place the trough among the trees. He'd then construct a fence in order to protect his garden.

Feeding wild deer was illegal in Colorado and, technically, the ones that had been coming into the garden should have been spooked by the presence of a human. Instead they'd wandered in as if they'd owned the place, which was a sure sign that someone, probably tourists, had been feeding them. But he needed to keep them away from the garden otherwise they'd treat it as a running buffet. He'd face off with the local wildlife officers if and when he had to.

Eating outside was something that he'd yet to do at Christmas Cottage. The weather had been nice but there had been nowhere suitable. With his butt resting on the low wall that ran alongside the cottage, Jay ate his oatmeal while fluffy white clouds meandered across the sky. It was perfect and peaceful. Almost too perfect and peaceful and Jay found it a struggle to get himself to go back inside and into the shower.

Once he was in work clothes, Jay put Blue into his harness and went back to the garden. He hammered a stake into the ground and attached the free end of Blue's leash to it. The cat just sat and stared at him before giving Jay a long, slow blink. Smiling, he bent down and scratched the cat's ears.

"See? You'll like it out here. You just can't go wandering off 'cause you won't come back. You'll either find friends, or get eaten by them."

Blue gave him a low, throaty meow before curling his paws beneath him and settling in the sun.

Fetching his tools from the small wooden shed, Jay set to work on the planters. The garden was brightly lit and the smell of a world coming back to life invigorated him. He lived for those moments. Lived for the times when he could feel *alive* and at one with the world around them. Using his hands and putting something together bought him immense joy and Jay spent the moments out in the sun going over the times that he'd been in that position before. Restoring old cars – check. Repairing and rebuilding guitars – check. Rebuilding the cottage's bedroom balcony – check. There was so much more that he wanted to do to the cottage. The roof was in need of being looked at and, at some point during the warmer weather, the chimney would need sweeping. That was a job that Jay was determined to do himself. Buy some brushes, watch a few videos, and hope that Dominic and Blue didn't get in the way. Cleaning a sooty Dominic would be easy. Jay didn't even want to think about trying to wrangle the cat into the shower.

By and large, the assembled planters weren't too heavy. They were, however, cumbersome and after trying to move one into place Jay decided to leave it until Dominic was home. Spare hands would be a blessing and he didn't want to spend the rest of the day laid up in front of the fire with more pulled muscles.

Once the three planters were done, he scooped up Blue and headed inside. He made coffee and fixed both the cat and himself something to eat. He was leaning against the kitchen counter and watching Blue trail his leash around the floor when he felt his phone ringing.

Dominic's name scrolled across the screen and Jay frowned as he answered it. He hadn't expected to hear from Dominic in the middle of the day.

"Hey. You okay?"

"Yeah. Yeah." The younger man sounded breathless. "I'm fine. I'm just getting the train to Boston. The *train*, Jay! I haven't been on a train in years. But it's the quickest route up there." Dominic paused and Jay could hear the sounds of a station around him. Echoing announcements and the tick, wheezing clatter of steel wheels on rails. "Anyway, I just wanted to let you know that I was thinking about you."

Jay smiled and let himself relax. "Thanks. I was thinking about you, too, but probably not in the way you think I'd be thinking about you."

"So not sweaty and naked? Dammit, Hammond. I call you up expecting dirty talk. Instead I get you talking normally to me."

Laughing felt good and Jay slid himself down to the floor of the kitchen. Once his knees were pulled up, Blue hopped into his lap and made himself comfortable.

With a hand on the cat's back, he replied, "Well, you'd be sweaty. And you can get naked afterwards. And, if you're really good, I'll scrub your back in the shower."

"Sounds good," Dominic purred. "What do you want help with?"

"Moving some planters. That's all."

"I can do that in exchange for a hot shower with you." An announcement blared out dangerously close to the phone. "Gotta go. My train's here. I'll be thinking about you while I'm rolling up to Boston. Call you later, okay?"

"Talk to you later, Dominic. Love you."

"Love you more."

And then the younger man was gone. Jay smiled at his phone before bending to kiss Blue's head. They sat for a few minutes longer, just savouring the silence and stillness, before Jay pulled himself back to his feet.

"Come on, cat. Let's get finished."

~~~

He built the planter on the opposite side of the low wall. Hidden by the trees, Jay hoped that it wouldn't be found by the authorities, at least not until he'd moved it further enough away from his property. Once it was finished, he placed a call to the animal feed wholesalers and ordered several bags of deer feed. He hoped that it would keep the over-friendly animals happy and away from his flourishing garden.

Fallen twigs and dead leaves rustled and Jay looked towards the sound. Eyes watched him and, after a few moments, the small herd of deer wandered from the trees. Jay smiled and pointed to the planter.

"This will be full tomorrow. Then you don't have to

come into the garden."

Large, furry ears flicked to listen to his voice and a couple took a few, tentative steps closer.

"No snacks out here. Sorry."

Jay was sure that the deer had no concept of the word "No". Whoever had been feeding them before they turned up on his doorstep had given them whatever they wanted. And they were determined that such a tradition should be followed.

The young fawn from a few days prior stepped forward and once more shoved her head into his hands. Jay grinned and stroked her slender face. She didn't seem to have a care in the world and just licked at his palms.

"After some salt, huh? I'll see if I can sneak a couple of salt blocks in there too."

The deer left once they realised that Jay wasn't going to lead them back to the house and whatever snacks sat in his cupboards. Truth be told, he needed to get to the store. Dominic would be home and demanding food in a few days.

Jay added getting his driver's license and a new truck to the ever growing list of things that he wanted, or needed, to do. His license had originally been taken away due to the DUI that landed him in rehab. Once he was out and at Christmas Cottage, he'd decided not to renew it. Everything was in walking distance and he could easily carry most things. Anything else he just ordered for delivery.

Except that he had Dominic to think of now.

Normally Dominic did the grocery shopping while he was at work. He'd close up Between the Sheets for an hour, grab a coffee from Joe's, and then idle around the grocery store. He'd always pick everything that was on the list, along with anything that was on sale, high in sugar, or could be eaten with one hand.

Downing a coffee and one of the snacks that he'd managed to keep away from the deer, Jay put on his walking boots and grabbed the rucksack. A pitiful meow from the stairs told him that someone else wanted to join him for a walk.

Sighing, Jay leaned against the bannister and looked at the cat. "I'm going shopping. Because we're nearly out of food and your friend, the one that eats as much as you do, will be coming home."

Blue gave him a forlorn look before jumping up onto the polished wood handrail. He tucked his head beneath Jay's chin and gave another sad meow.

Feeling himself cave, Jay kissed the cat's head and went to find his harness. Strapping it around the cat, he said, "You can ride on my shoulders on the way into town but you're walking on the way home. I can't carry food *and* you."

Jay sighed and stared down at his big, grey cat. He wasn't quite sure how much Blue understood. He definitely knew a lot of words. Like "Food", "Water", "Walk", and "Dominic". Jay was sure that Blue knew more than he let on and, like any cat, just chose to ignore whatever came out of his owner's mouth.

The trees felt like a break away from all that life

threw at him. They were where he escaped to in the early days of his rehab. The forest that had surrounded the rehab centre in northern California had been a break away from all that was happening within him. They'd cradled him against their trunks and soothed him with the soft whispers of a breeze through leaves. In those moments, he'd been able to forget about why he was in rehab and just feel calm.

Those days were long behind him and, for that, Jay was glad. The pain that he'd endured while fighting addictions and coming out of the closet had pushed him so close to the edge. Stepping off and into the void would have been so easy. Yet something had kept him on the straight and narrow and pushed him to find the cottage. Maybe, just maybe, there was something more to their world than merely existing.

There was a big box supermarket on the outskirts of Waybridge. But with Blue in tow, it was too far to walk. So the smaller place in the centre of town would have to do. Not that Jay minded. The walk was beautiful and Waybridge's gently sloping Main Street gave great views of the surrounding scenery. Plus it was a chance for Blue to get all the attention that he wanted from locals and tourists alike.

The grocery store was always busy and Jay waved to the young staff as he entered. With Blue still perched on his shoulders, he wandered the aisles, picking up the food that he'd need for the coming days. He really did like the store. It was small enough to feel homely while being large enough to lose himself in. The music was instrumental rather than an in-store radio and the lighting wasn't as harsh as the chain places that he'd otherwise visit.

Experience had taught him that the bakery aisle was Dominic's favourite. The dark-haired man often came home with a crumpled paper bag of reduced pastries and a happy smile on his face. The little things honestly were the ones that made him happy and Jay wasn't going to deny them to Dominic even if copious amounts of cinnamon rolls were unhealthy.

A chill settled over him as he stood before the array of freshly baked goods. Their smell may have been tempting him but the sight of piles of pastries made him feel suddenly ill.

What if Dominic was cheating on him? What if New York and Boston were a good excuse to escape for a while? Dominic had taken a chance that Jay wouldn't suspect a thing if he left with several empty suitcases. But what if he did return with full cases of wares? Would that mean that Dominic had somehow staged everything in order to have a fling in a far-off city?

With his stomach in knots, Jay drifted towards the checkout. The young man that served him smiled and addressed him by name. Jay gave him a tight smile and greeted him in return. He accepted treats for Blue and packed everything into his rucksack. His head continued to pound as he left the store and stepped back out into the clear mountain air.

Yet the reminder of Dominic was still there. To his

left was the darkened shop with its handwritten sign still hanging in the window. Jay didn't give it another thought as he found the shop's spare key on his own keychain and let himself in.

The air in Between the Sheets was still. Dust danced in the early spring sunlight and the shelves were indeed looking forlornly empty. Rounding the counter, Jay dropped Blue onto the wooden surface and began to poke around. The till was empty as he'd expected it would be and the screen of the cordless phone flashed to indicate several new voice mails. Jay decided not to check them instead turning to his attention to the shelves beneath the counter.

A handful of papers were stacked to one side and an old take out coffee cup sat beside them. Other than that, the shelves were empty.

Jay didn't even know what he was looking for. Evidence of Dominic's infidelity? A sign that the younger man wasn't all that interested in him? Getting back to his feet, Jay moved to the small kitchen-cum-stockroom. Everything was spotless and even the coffee machine had been emptied and cleaned. Dominic had known for a while that he'd be leaving for several days.

In a nook beneath the stairs was a small desk with a laptop and printer. Both were off but a single sheet of paper sat on the printer. Picking it up, Jay read the short message.

I have what you're looking for. See you on the East Coast.

– *Andreas*

Chapter 8

Spring's first storm rumbled across the heavens but Jay had decided not to enjoy it. Seated on the couch, he stared at the piece of paper in his hands. His heart felt like a lump of rock and another felt as though it was wedged in his throat. His mind was as dark as the clouds that currently lingered in the skies. Sensing Jay's mood, Blue had gone and hidden himself in the kitchen window, presumably to watch the rain.

The email was crumpled from where he'd screwed it up in frustration and anger. Jay knew that he should never have questioned his intuition and that Dominic, like so many others, would eventually give up on him and walk. Dominic had probably wanted someone who was a little less paranoid and had fewer issues. Hell, he'd probably gone back to the guy he'd been with before he'd moved to Waybridge.

Jay dashed off a quick text. *Who's Andreas?*

He decided to omit his usual "The fuck is" in the hope that the two words wouldn't panic Dominic too much. He wanted to speak to the younger man. Wanted to find out what was going on. At the same time, he had to keep his anger under control. Shouting would solve nothing because he truly did love Dominic and wanted him to come home. He just wanted answers.

His heart skipped as his phone began to ring. Dominic's name scrolled across the screen and Jay felt his breath hitch as he swiped to answer.

"You've been to the shop, haven't you?"

Dominic was out in the street somewhere in Boston. His hair was windswept and the collar of his black coat was pulled up against the sea breeze. His face was lined not with anger but with worry.

"Yeah." Jay sighed as the anger melted from him. Suddenly he felt guilty for prying into Dominic's life. "Yeah, I have."

"And you weren't just checking on it, were you? Which would be sweet, by the way."

He shook his head and sank further into the couch. "Sorry," he murmured. "I shouldn't have gone looking."

"You're worried that I'm cheating on you?" The image jumped as Dominic walked only to settle when the younger man seated himself on a bench. A tree was visible just over his shoulder as was a digital bus schedule.

The guilt grew, his stomach churning as the metaphorical rock tumbled through it. "Yeah, I was."

"You've managed to convince yourself that I am so that you can justify any actions if and when I leave or we have an argument?"

Jay nodded and looked down at his fingers. Tattoos, faded with time, were etched into his knuckles and there was still a hairless line around his ring finger.

"I'm not leaving you, Jay. I don't know what I need to do to convince you that I'm not going anywhere but I'll figure it out." Dominic shrugged, sighed and ran a hand through his hair. "I don't know. Take you on every buying trip. Wear a GPS tracker. Marry you. I don't know but I'll figure it, okay."

"I'm sorry." Jay sighed and straightened himself up. He took a deep breath. Dominic deserved more than a pitiful plea. "I'm sorry. I shouldn't have done what I did. I shouldn't be prying into your life. And I shouldn't be allowing my brain to go down those roads."

"Hey. Hey. Listen to me, Jay. I understand. Well, most of it anyway. You're pretty much fresh out of rehab *and* fresh out of the closet. Shit's going to weird you out for a long time and I've gotta be prepared for that, too. I'm chill. You know this. I take life as it happens and you're not going to weird me out by going on the occasional "Dominic's cheating on me" ride. Going into my store to look for evidence, yes, that's gonna piss me off. Going in there to check on it and make sure no-one's done the place over, no. That's sweet and I appreciate that. But going in there and taking the email that I forgot to pick up from the printer isn't a great look. Everything else I can deal with. You-"

Unable to help himself, Jay interrupted the dark-haired man. "You've got to let me apologise!"

"And you have. I forgive you. However, if you want to do something else, you can always take me out when I get home. There's that new Italian place down by the river that I've been meaning to check out."

Jay knew the one. Painfully expensive and with a

list of glittering reviews as long as the river. But he could afford it and, as far as he was concerned, Dominic was worth it.

"And about Andreas." There were times when Dominic just didn't shut up. Jay enjoyed the quiet moments but he also enjoyed hearing his lover's voice, especially when he was at full throttle. "He helped me to track down a very specific piece of music. It's one that you heard and, because I know you play piano, I thought it would be a nice gift. It's been out of print for about twenty years. He's one of my dealers and, like any good music dealer, he knew someone who had a copy for sale. So there you go. Was going to be a surprise but you couldn't help yourself."

Jay glanced at the screen and found that Dominic had broken out into his trademark million watt smile.

"Just a warning for the next time you go prying, Hammond."

A smile broke his own stony expression and Jay melted back against the couch. "Thank you. I love you."

"Love you, too. Feeling better?"

Jay nodded. The digital numbers above Dominic's head ticked over. "Should be letting you go. It's nearly a meal time."

"I know. I was going to head to a burger joint I spotted a few blocks back. Grab something there and head back to the hotel for the night. Call you when I get in?"

"I'd love that, thanks."

Dominic nodded before an expression of surprise crossed his face. "Look, Jay!"

He flipped to the back camera just as a white and yellow bus pulled in with a wheezing hiss.

"We don't see those in Waybridge. At least not very often."

Jay chuckled as he watched people step off the bus and others step on. "Careful, Grohl. You're acting like a tourist now."

"Hey, when in Rome." The camera flipped back around to Dominic's smiling, and slightly flushed, face. "See you in a while, okay?"

"See you soon, Dominic. Love you."

"Love you, too, baby. Go and enjoy a shower and something to eat. I'll catch you later."

Jay felt himself begin to settle as darkness fell. There was something about the coming of the night that made things a little easier. Life was resting and, with it, the cottage also quietened. Eventually he found himself curled up on the couch with yet another battered paperback and the cat for company. The memory of his fears was becoming just that... a distant memory.

How did he become so lucky to have hooked up with Dominic? To have found someone who accepted that there would be bumps in the metaphorical road and mentally prepared himself for them? Dominic himself had said that he'd been mad about Jay going into Between the Sheets. But he'd also expressed understanding for why Jay had done it. And rather than get angry, he'd taken the time to explain who the mystery man was.

Jay stretched out and rested his ankles on the opposite couch arm. Blue had wedged himself between his human and the cushions and was purring up a storm as another one rolled in outside. Rain pattered against the windows and thunder rolled overhead. Shivers tickled along Jay's spine and he pulled the blanket from the back of the couch down onto his legs.

"Perfect," he murmured to Blue. "This is absolutely perfect." Placing the book on the floor, Jay rested a hand on Blue's back and closed his eyes. "Do you remember that it was like this when we first moved in? Rain didn't give up for days. But, man, was it worth it."

He drifted in and out of sleep for the best part of an hour. Deciding that he couldn't do with waking up with *another* bad back, Jay eventually dragged himself from the couch and to bed. As per usual, Blue was hot on his heels.

Jay shed his clothes and eased himself beneath the heavy bed covers. There was a safety to the weight that he enjoyed and, with his hands hooked behind his head, Jay looked around himself. The bed was flanked by two small side tables, each holding a lamp and whatever the other man needed. Jay's had a pair of glasses, another book, and a glass of water. Dominic's, on the other hand, was a towering mass of books, odd papers, glasses that he'd forgotten about, and half drunk glasses of water. Another of the several long charging cables that he owned snaked its way around the Art Deco style lamp.

Hanging above the bed was a framed print of the mountains that surrounded Waybridge. Jay had found it in the town's art gallery and fallen in love. The photograph and an *All Guests Must Be Approved By The Cat* sign that hung beside the front door were the only pieces of art that he possessed.

~~~

The deer food arrived the next morning and Jay wasted no time in dragging a bag into the trees. He hadn't even finished filling the trough before the sound of animals moving through the trees reached his ears. Looking up, he found the small herd standing a few feet away with their eyes firmly trained on him.

"Look!" He grinned and gestured to the wooden feeder. "Now you don't have to come to the door every day. And if I ever find out who'd been feeding you, I'll kill them. Because they shouldn't have been doing that."

He stepped out of the way and watched as the deer trotted up and stuck their noses in to the pile of pellets. With a satisfied smile, Jay left them to their breakfast and returned to the cottage for his own.

By and large, he'd slept well. The bed had held him in a warm cocoon and Blue had snored softly beside his head. As morning had dawned so Jay had woken feeling like a new man. The worries that he'd had the previous day were melting to nothing. All that he had to do was keep Dominic beside him. That was a worry that he'd have to address once the younger man returned home because what Jay had done wasn't acceptable. Allowing his fears to take over and seep into his relationship was setting a dangerous precedent for future control. And he refused to be the one to allows his issues to restrict Dominic's movements and see the younger man be in any kind of pain.

"Keep working on it, Jay," he murmured as he prepared coffee. "Dominic understood this time around. Don't know if he'd be so forgiving next time."

Sitting at the table, Jay browsed Pickens' website as he drank. While he had most of what he wanted to plant, the other part of the plan was to buy ready-grown flowers and put them in the flowerbeds. At least until the following year when they could be planted up with bulbs.

After twenty minutes of perusing flowers, he flicked over to finding an awning for the back. Somewhere to sit when it was raining and they couldn't be bothered to head for the trees. Jay found one that he liked and, deciding that it would be Dominic's project to install, he put it in his shopping basket.

Next up was a bench for beneath the trees and he found a ready-built one with a rolled back and arms.

Into the basket it went.

The bench and awning were closely followed by bird feeders, bird food, and a quote for the pond that he wanted.

He'd burned through a pot of coffee and nearly two hours by the time he was finished. The sun was shimmering through the windows and the air was holding that early Spring feeling to it. Looking around the cottage, Dominic debated how he could make it more homely. More art? More furniture? He didn't want to go over the top and he was by no means materialistic.

His eyes came to rest on the guitar. He'd left it out and leaning against a chair with the case on the floor beside it. Wrapping his hand around the neck, Jay picked up the guitar and dropped himself onto the couch. He nestled the guitar against his knees and began to softly play.

Music had the power to heal, to soothe, and to transport both musician and listener off to another world. As always, Jay found that happening as chords that were once so familiar to him fell from the guitar. The world as he knew it became nothing and the worries that had blackened his soul withered and died. His life was perfect and he had all that he'd ever dreamed of. Now all he had to to was keep everything in order. No more fucking up. No more irrational fears. No more lashing out at those he loved because he believed that they were doing all they could to harm him.

Eventually Jay put the guitar to one side and heaved himself back to his feet. He smiled warmly at the instrument and felt the serenity of knowing that all would be well settle back over him.

Changing into some work clothes, Jay made his way back to the garden. He had a ball of string and some stakes in hand and an excited cat chittering at his feet. Blue had always been an indoor cat, even back at his old house. For him to now feel soil beneath his paws and to smell the clear air must have been sensory overload. But Blue was more than happy to sit with his leash wrapped around a stake and chatter to the birds.

Jay's mind turned to Dominic as he marked out the areas of the garden. The younger man would be home in a couple of days and the silence of the cottage would be broken once more. Not that Jay minded. He wouldn't have invited Dominic into his space if he wasn't prepared to live with the other man's personality.

But he did worry that Dominic was becoming all that he thought about and that codependency was beginning to inch its way into his life. As far as he was concerned, he'd found the partner that he'd always wanted. But – there was always a but. With it came the old habits and one of those was trying to keep the people he loved as close to him as possible.

"Maybe I need to get some therapy again," he murmured. "Try and iron this out before it becomes too much of a problem."

Straightening up, he pulled his phone from his pocket and was surprised to find a text from Dominic. Normally the younger man was blowing up his phone, although that only tended to happen when Dominic was having a slow day. Put him somewhere busy and Dominic appeared to forget that anyone else existed.

Even in the midst of an obviously hectic shopping spree, Dominic had found a moment to pause and text him. Jay smiled as he unlocked the phone and found a photo of the sea.

Needed some air and took a walk. We need to come here one day. Love you. Xx

His intention had been to look for a local therapist but Dominic's note had stopped him in his tracks. Making his way up to the trees in the corner of the garden plot, Jay stood and took a photo of the newly worked ground.

He replied with, *The garden right now. Going to look beautiful when it's done*, he replied. *Love you, too. Xx*

Chapter 9

A therapist still wasn't a bad idea and Jay found himself one in the centre of Waybridge. Clara had a studio above a clothing shop just a stone's throw from The Book Nook. Which meant that it was also close to Between the Sheets. Jay knew that Dominic wouldn't mind him having therapy; heck, they'd spoken about it often enough. But he did worry that the proximity to Dominic may cause him to express himself less than he normally would. Still, there was no harm in trying.

Jay made an introductory appointment to see if they were a good fit for the following day. After that he'd decided to take himself on a date to the Stone Bridge Inn. He hadn't been back since they'd had their first unofficial "date" there so many months before. Jay remembered the restaurant with fondness and wanted to grasp some of those initial feelings once more. He also hoped that it would remind of why he fell in love with Dominic. Of seeing those dark eyes light up. Of seeing that smile tug at the other's lips. Of seeing him fidget through nervousness.

The memories warmed Jay as he went about his day. Other than the garden, there really wasn't much that needed doing. There was the odd patch of dust and he really did need to get the stepladder out and clean the chandelier. But they could wait for another day.

Jay felt as though he was feathering his nest. He

was making it homely for the one that he loved. And it was a strange feeling that he'd never really experienced before. Sure, he'd done the same with his wife but it had never impacted him as much as it did in that moment. Yet doing it for Dominic felt more meaningful.

He laid another fire ready for the evening before making a coffee and crashing onto the couch. His body was sore with the aches of a long day but Jay was satisfied with all that he'd achieved. Blue hopped up beside him and, for a few moments, Jay allowed himself to bathe in the silence of the cottage.

The cottage really was perfect and Jay was glad that he'd had the opportunity to purchase it. Buried among the trees, the little house truly was an escape from the outside world. A place for him to rest his head and just *breathe*.

He idled through the rest of the day, cleaning and tidying the cottage. By the time night began to fall, he was dusty and sweaty and the cottage was spotlessly clean. Jay hauled himself into the shower before collapsing into bed with Blue and a novel about a New York cop. He was just getting engrossed in the story when his phone vibrated on the bedside table. Other than the occasional phone call from his kids or the band, there was only one other person who called him, especially at such a later hour.

Without even looking at the phone, Jay swiped to answer. "Hey, Dominic."

Dominic's face, along with his trademark megawatt smile, came into view on the screen. "How did you know it was me?"

"Who else would it be at this time of night?"

Dominic was obviously sat in his hotel room. His profile was reflected in the large window and Jay could see the faint outline of the Boston skyline. "True. True. How are you doing?"

"Comfortable. Reading," Jay replied with a smile.

"Did I disturb you?" Dominic's face became a little pained. "I know that you enjoy your quiet time."

His heart melted at Dominic's worried words. "You never disturb me. Ever. In fact, I love it when you disturb me. You remind me that I need to live in the now and not in my head."

Dominic took a sip of soda before setting the can down on a table that Jay couldn't see. The younger man flicked his hair over his shoulders before shuffling deeper into the chair. "You know, it's nice to hear that. I know I don't often talk about it, but you know that sometimes my confidence ain't great. It's been beaten and battered and knocked around. Watching your younger boyfriend leave you for someone younger than you. Having another call you useless in bed."

Tears prickled Jay's eyes and he reached out to touch a finger to the small phone screen. He could hear the pain in Dominic's voice and so desperately wanted to help him.

"I wish you'd told me while you were here," he whispered.

Dominic swallowed hard enough for Jay to see his Adam's apple move. The dark-haired man shook his head and averted his gaze.

"I wish you were here, Dominic. I wish you weren't opening your soul up over the phone. I love you. You know that, right?"

Dominic nodded and his shoulders rose and fell. The phone shook a little in his hand.

"And," Jay continued, "for the record, I wouldn't leave. And I'd definitely never call you useless in bed."

"But you've never been with another man," Dominic softly protested.

"And? I don't want to be with another man. I want to be with you." Jay sighed. He could see that Dominic was getting into a funk and that there would probably be no way to pull him out of it. Dominic needed to do that himself. "Come home. Please."

They talked until Dominic looked ready to fall asleep. Jay refused to let him go any earlier. He was worried for Dominic and wanted to make sure that the younger man was okay before hanging up.

With his hands linked behind his head, Jay stared at the ceiling. His heart was breaking for Dominic. There was so much pain that he had never heard about. Pain that had come from previous relationships and which Dominic had buried deep. And Jay understood why. All of them wanted to be viewed as fun-loving and outgoing. No-one wanted to be seen as the person who carried a black cloud around with them.

Night may have been wearing on but Jay found himself drawn from the bed. Driven by the emotions of the call, he began to empty and rearrange the closet and drawers. Dominic's clothes and belongings were dotted around the cottage, stashed in any old corner. Taking each piece that he found, Jay folded or hung it in the correct place. He wanted Dominic to feel at home and not just as a partner who passed by and, when the sun rose, went on his merry way. He wanted the younger man to feel secure, and loved, and, most importantly, seen. He wanted Dominic to know that he always had a home to come back to.

Jay worked until the early hours before falling back into bed. The bedroom, small as it already was, looked better. Neater. Tidier. There weren't several boxes pushed up against the handrail and Dominic's small pile of clothes had disappeared from beside the bed. He'd also made a note to buy Dominic a small bookcase for his ever growing book pile.

Blue was curled on the opposite pillow with his sleepy amber eyes firmly trained on Jay.

"What?" Jay asked with a shrug. "I'm only trying to make the place a little better. Stop judging me." Laughing, he leaned across the bed and gave the cat a kiss. "And your friend will be home soon. I promise."

Jay slept deeply. There were no anxiety riddled dreams and nothing to wake him in the middle of the night. He eventually woke to the sun streaming through the cottage and Blue purring loudly beside him. With a smile on his lips, he rolled over and hugged his cat close.

"Hungry?"

Blue's purring just became louder and the cat wriggled free. There was the thud of paws on the floor before Blue turned on the howling. Dragging himself from the bed, he jokingly shouted at Blue to be quiet before racing the cat down the stairs. As always, his ever hungry feline beat him into the kitchen and was already sitting beside his bowl as Jay took the last step.

"At least you keep me fit, cat. I suppose I should be grateful for that. Just wish you wouldn't wake the dead every morning."

Once the cat was fed, Jay filled a travel mug with coffee, grabbed the half empty sack of deer feed and made his way outside.

The morning was beautiful with clear blue skies and crisp air. The freshly turned soil smelled of spring and fresh life. Birds sang in the trees and, beyond the cottage, he heard a car rumble by. His heart was singing and Jay felt as though he was at one with the land. The mountains had embraced him as their own and their grasp on him would last for the rest of his days.

Shadows dappled the forest floor and the bag caught on a knot of rock. Pausing, Jay tugged it free and continued to the small feeder. The coffee awakened his senses and he couldn't help but sing softly as he poured the pellets into the trough.

Just as the last of the feed rattled against the wood, Jay heard animals shuffling through the undergrowth. His smile only widened as he turned and found the deer standing behind him. All of them were staring at him with expectant looks on their faces.

"Breakfast is served!" he exclaimed before stepping out of the way.

The smaller deer trotted forward and stuck their noses in before their older friends followed. Jay parked himself on a fallen tree and drank his coffee while he watched them. He knew that he shouldn't be feeding them. But they'd keep turning up at his door if he didn't. And he was going to get to the bottom of why they were turning up at the cottage.

Those early hours were peaceful. Sitting with his travel mug on his knees, Jay felt far more relaxed than he had done in a long time. A gentle breeze tickled his ankles and the back of his neck while the soft sound of deer eating filled the air.

The day was perfect for doing something and, for the first time in a long time, Jay decided to dedicate it to himself. He'd do whatever he wanted. Take a walk. Have multiple cups of coffee in the soon-to-be garden. Take himself on a date. Deep down, he knew that he needed to look after himself. That his soul was crying out for something more than the mere company of another person. He needed to love himself as much as he loved Dominic.

With that in mind, Jay went inside and tossed himself in the shower with the plan of booking a table at Angelo's. It was *the* restaurant that Dominic wanted to try but, and he felt a little selfish for it, Jay had decided that it would be the place for him to go and treat himself.

But first, and with a stone in his gut, he made his way down into Waybridge's centre for his first appointment with Clara.

Her office was spacious and calm. Jay liked calm. The walls were white and the windows overlooked the scenery of Main Street and the mountains in the distance. One corner was a veritable forest of plants and the sweet smell of lemongrass came from what he assumed was a hidden defuser.

Clara herself was a middle-aged lady with long, chestnut brown hair and warm green eyes. She invited him to sit on the surprisingly comfortable couch before moving to sit across from him.

Her voice was as soft as her face, "Jay, it's a pleasure to meet you."

Hunched forward so as to hide his tall frame, Jay smiled. "Goes both ways."

"Why don't you tell me why you're here and we'll see if we can work together." She leaned back in her chair and folded her hands across her lap.

Jay nodded and took a deep breath. His life was varied and often confusing. Family issues that had left him scarred and had landed him in rehab the first time around. Stress and memories which had triggered his most recent in-patient stay. And, of course, the issues that were now flaring around his relationship with Dominic.

And so he began. Jay started at the beginning and worked his way through growing up with a dysfunctional family before moving onto music and Winter Angels. He detailed his first stint in rehab, the band's comeback, and his second trip down the alcoholic rabbit hole. Clara appeared interested as he told her about leaving everything behind in order to start afresh in Waybridge. He told her about the cottage, Blue, and about meeting Dominic. Jay finished up by telling her of his recent issues and of looking for reasons that Dominic would leave.

Finally, and with little energy left, Jay allowed himself to relax back into the couch and stretch his out his legs.

Clara looked at him for a moment before speaking. "You've had an interesting life, Jay. One that, as you said, most people would want if they didn't know about all that you'd been through. I would be honoured to help you find the peace and security that you want. Although it sounds as though you're already making some headway by speaking to Dominic about all that's happening with you right now."

Jay nodded and glanced out of the window. "He's a good soul but I do worry that one day he'll tire of whatever issues come to light."

"Well, maybe one day we can approach that with Dominic."

A bird soared past the window and he turned back

to her with a smile. "That would be good." Jay paused before he sighed. "Thank you. I really appreciate this."

And he did. Being able to talk about all that had happened, and was still happening, soothed his soul and his aching brain. He made another appointment, thanked Clara again, and left with a spring in his step. Life truly was looking up.

Chapter 10

Jay took himself home for a shower and a change of clothes before he headed out to Angelo's. Oh, and there was the issue of a very hungry cat, too. There was no way that he could leave Blue for another few hours without a meal. He would likely come home to a wrecked house and a smug looking cat.

He dressed himself in grey pants, a white shirt, and a grey waistcoat. Looking and feeling good was part of the experience and he didn't want to turn up with his silver hair tied in his neck and wearing a pair of gardening jeans.

"Lookin' good, Hammond." Jay smiled at himself in the mirror.

There was a pressure at his ankles and he looked down to find Blue curling around his legs. His smile widened and he reached down to stroke the cat.

"Place is all yours for a couple of hours. Look after it, okay?"

Blue gave him a soft meow before sticking his claws into the weave of the pants. Jay hissed as the sharp points caught in his skin but he made no move to shoo the cat away.

As he crossed narrow road and made his way back into the trees, Jay seriously began to debate getting a car once more. His license had been suspended following his alcohol related crash and, in the intervening months, he'd felt no need to get it back. He'd moved to a place where he could roam freely on foot, which was something that he'd always wanted. But he was finding that he was having make several trips a day back and forth to the cottage, an issue that would make having a car worthwhile.

He broke through the trees and onto Main Street. Weaving through tourists and locals alike, Jay took a narrow, cobbled side street. The tiny street, which was no more than a pathway, split a building in two. On the left was one of Waybridge's many cafe and on the right was a store specialising in high end clothing.

Coming out the other side, Jay found himself standing on the banks of the river. Trees clung to the rocky face and the water raced over millennia-beaten stones. The sound was soothing and the air around it was the freshest he'd find in the area. For a moment, he stood and filled himself with the tranquillity of the area. This was why he'd moved to Waybridge; the town's tiny size and the splendour of the scenery.

Lifting his head, he looked up at the mountains that soared up and away from the river. The tree line was clearly visible and the tops of the mountains appeared blue against the cloud-dappled sky. Beyond the clouds, the sky was beginning to show the first signs of sunset. Birds swung by on the thermals, dipping and diving before picking up the next gust of warm air.

Angelo's was just along the bank from the Stone Bridge Inn and Jay gave it a soft smile as he passed by. Like pretty much every other building in Waybridge, Angelo's was built in the Swiss chalet style. A balcony hung from the first floor and wood outlined the gables of the red-tiled roof.

Soft light drifted through the windows and Jay felt his shoulders drop a little as he walked through the front door. He was greeted by a suited waiter with a big smile and an Italian accent and taken to a booth with a view of the forest. Wooden beams criss-crossed the ceiling with curved iron light fittings hanging from the joints.

He was nicely secluded away from anyone watching. Not that they would. Waybridge had proved time and again that it was the kind of place that people like himself, people who'd garnered some level of recognition, could live comfortably and without the fear of being hassled on every street.

Picking up the menu, Jay scanned over the drinks list. He skipped the wines and beers and headed straight for the soda. He settled on sparkling water with a twist of lime and jumped straight into the list of mouthwatering foods.

"Are you ready to order, sir?"

Snapped from his thoughts, Jay looked up to see a middle-aged man standing before him. Like the waiter who'd greeted him at the door, this one also wore the seemingly traditional black suit and white shirt of waiters. He gave Jay a small smile.

"Yeah. Sure. Can I get a sparkling water with a twist of lime to drink."

"Certainly. And for your meal?"

Jay glanced back to the menu. "The Zio Nino,

please."

The waiter nodded. "Excellent choice. I'll be back shortly with your drink."

Settling back into the booth, Jay stared out of the window and to the trees beyond the glass. Dominic, he'd decided, would love this little corner of the town. If anything, it would help to ease the other man's occasional energetic outbursts. He took his phone out and snapped a photograph of the nearly empty restaurant and sent it to Dominic. As it was early evening there were only a few other diners, possibly tourists who were hoping to get a pleasant meal in before any crowds arrived. It was perfect and Jay could feel himself relaxing.

He had to smile at Dominic's reply a moment later. *You're eating with ME?! Traitor!*

Jay grinned. **Don't worry. I'll bring you here. I think I'm on a promise anyway.**

Damn right you will. This weekend?

How about next week?

They went back and forth for several minutes until Jay's drink arrived. He smiled and nodded at the waiter and sent one final text to Dominic before putting his phone down. He knew that he'd pick it up once his food arrived in order to send Dominic another taunting photograph.

A gentle breeze rustled through the pine trees outside of the restaurant and Jay settled back to watch them. He sipped on his drink and a smile twitched at his lips. Happy and content; that's what he was. He'd finally found someone to settle down with. As the sky continued to darken so his reflection made an appearance in the window. Jay's hair was curled into the nap of his neck and as much as he protested about cutting it, Dominic would hear nothing of the sort. Dominic appeared to like men with long, silver hair and, for the time being, Jay was allowing him to live out his fantasy.

The same went with his body. Dominic really couldn't get enough of him and Jay made very few moves to stop him. Whenever he did, his quiet protests were silenced with gentle kisses before Dominic curled up beside him. Boundaries, at least, were respected between them. He let Dominic go down internet-fuelled rabbit holes and Dominic would try (and fail) to initiate sex when Jay was too tired to participate.

Jay knew that he had to work on his portly figure. Although, with Dominic's help, he'd come to love and accept himself more than he had a year prior. Everything would happen in its own time. It always had and everything had always worked out for the best. His band and Dominic were proof of that. Heck, even his own life was proof that things would come up trumps for him.

His meal arrived and Jay had to stop himself from drooling. The meatballs were sitting in a rich tomato sauce with a bed of spaghetti beneath them. The smell was divine and Jay snapped another photo before digging in. Over his own soft moans of appreciation he could hear his phone chirruping with Dominic's indignant replies.

As with every restaurant visit, the food was far better than anything he himself cooked. The meal that evening, if he'd bothered cooking, would have been something he'd had in the freezer or another takeout. Jay had only really seriously started to cook once Dominic had started hanging around. Before then his meals had been basic; whatever he could make a pan of and freeze the leftovers.

The food at Angelo's was heavenly and he knew that Dominic was going to swoon over it. The younger man would probably head straight into steak territory but Jay hoped that he'd stretch his wings and try something a little different. But then Dominic was a barbecue man. He'd cooked it for a living and the marinades obviously ran through his veins.

Once he'd finished eating, Jay ordered a coffee and sat back to enjoy the ambiance. Through the window he could see clouds slowly rolling over the mountains and blocking out the otherwise starry night. An involuntary shiver ran down his spine and he checked the weather app. A band of ran did appear to be drifting ever closer and, as much as he liked the rain, Jay didn't have any desire to be caught out in it. Spring, and the showers that came with it, had well and truly settled in.

Draining the last of the coffee, he paid the bill and left a generous tip. Once he'd made another booking for the following week, Jay thanked the staff and made his way out into the night.

The scent of rain was definitely hanging in the air, heavy and mossy and with an edge of damp. Walking back along the river, Jay took in the beauty of the evening. Fairy lights twinkled in every tree, a constant year round display that drew in tourists even when Christmas was long over. Main Street was the same with shop fronts and trees decorated with soft lights.

Even with the threat of rain in the air, Jay paused beneath one of the trees and marvelled at the lights as they swayed in the gentle breeze. Points of light that appeared to flicker in and out of existence as the branches moved.

Beneath him, the river continued to rush by, unhindered by time or man. The water crashed against the rugged bank and Jay could feel the spray when he took a step closer. It was refreshing after the cosy warmth of Angelo's.

Finally, he pulled himself away from the edge of the river and stepped back onto the path. No doubt there would be a hungry cat upon his return him. And, at some point, a call from Dominic to scold him for being the first to visit the new restaurant.

Waybridge was so quaint it was almost painful. Each building on Main Street mirrored its European counterparts with wood frames, gabled roofs, and windows large enough to allow a glimpse of the warm world inside. With Spring still inching its way in, many of the cafes, bars, and restaurants that were open still had log fires and candles burning. Jay ached to step into another in order to savour that safe little world but he knew that the telling off that he'd receive from Blue wouldn't be worth the small comfort he'd get. Besides, he had a fire and warm drinks at home.

He wound his way along the wide cobbled street and beneath the fairy-lit trees until he came to the tuning that would cut between a handful of buildings and take him into the forest. Jay walked carefully as his feet found soil. His eyes took a moment to adjust to the sudden darkness and he slowed his pace as he walked up the gentle slope. He could feel the forest coming back to life. Trees were beginning to bloom once more and the smell of fresh moss was rich in the air.

The first drop of rain caught the end of his nose and Jay muttered softly to himself. His head ached a little, a sign that the weather certainly was changing from the bright sunshine that had drenched the town earlier in the day.

A gentle drizzle had started to fall as he came out onto the road in front of the cottage. The porch light had come on automatically and Jay could see the fine rain in the glare of the bulb.

The light also illuminated something which made Jay both excited and a little fearful.

A small car sat on the driveway. A small car which, a few days earlier, had driven to the airport. And which should still have been at the airport, at least for a couple more days.

Taking his keys from his pocket, Jay walked across

the road and approached the cottage. Pausing on the step, he took a deep breath and composed himself. Inside was the man with whom he'd fallen in love with. The man who, despite Jay's own tantrum from a day prior, still proclaimed that he loved him.

Chapter 11

Finally, he opened the door and stepped in. A fire had been lit in the grate and a figure stood before it with Blue cradled in their arms. The image was enough to warm Jay and bring a smile to his face. The fear that he'd been feeling slowly melted away.

"Hey," he softly said. "Didn't expect you home so soon."

The figure moved and Jay took another step forward. Firelight rippled over the darkness of Dominic's hair and sank into the depths of his dark eyes. A pair of thick rimmed glasses held the hair from his face and Blue gave a soft *meow* when he spotted Jay.

"I'd done what I needed to do," Dominic replied with a shrug. "So I thought I'd hop on a plane and come home."

"I'm glad that you did." Jay's voice was barely a whisper as he crossed the living area.

He stopped before the fire and looked into the eyes of the man before him. No-one should be put on a pedestal and worshipped, but Jay felt as though he needed to do it for Dominic. The younger man was kind, patient, loving, and everything that Jay needed in order for him to come out of his shell. He forgave easily and loved even easier. He was a joy to be around and to keep him shackled and harnessed to the cottage would be to destroy the very being that Dominic was.

Reaching out, he stroked a hand down Dominic's cheek as though to reassure himself that the other man was truly real. A smile twitched at Dominic's lips before the younger man leaned in and gave him a kiss.

"I've missed you," Jay murmured.

Dominic's eyes sparkled in the fire light. "Kinda guessed that. Sorry for making you worry."

The warmth of the love that he held flooded through him and Jay stepped closer to wrap an arm around Dominic's neck. His fingers curled into the other man's long, dark hair. "Sorry for reacting the way I did."

"It happens. But it's nice to be home." Dominic shuffled a little closer, making sure not to trap Blue between them as he leaned against Jay. "I love being on the road but I've missed being here. Missed the fires. Missed the cat. Missed you."

They stood like that for a moment longer, savouring the silence and listening to the pop of the fire and the patter of the rain on the roof. Jay felt at peace in Dominic's presence as though everything had righted itself in the world. He knew that he still had issues that needed dealing with and he was determined to fix them.

"Seeing a therapist," he murmured.

That caused Dominic to pull back and he looked at the other man's frown. "Why?"

Jay sighed and rolled his head back. "Because I still obviously have issues. If this week's taught me anything it's that I'm more than a little codependent and probably slightly controlling. Controlling is good when it comes to my band. It's not so great when it comes to a relationship. I don't want you to feel as though you're being confined here or that you're having your wings clipped."

Fingers crept across his cheek and gently tugged his gaze back down to Dominic's. The younger man was still cradling Blue in one arm and was the image of gentleness and love.

"I don't think you're gonna try and contain me," Dominic softly replied. "Far from it. You're not one of those guys who's gonna tell me what to do. I love you for who you are and I appreciate that you're continuing to address issues from your past. A lot of other guys wouldn't do that. They'd have told me to shut the fuck up if I'd told them that I wasn't cheating. I'd have dreaded coming home. But, with you, I don't. I know you're sorry for what's happening and that you're trying to fix it. Doesn't mean I didn't already love you for you. Like we've said before, we all have issues, Jay. Every single one of us. I can be clingy, or needy, or, at times, just need to get out for a while. And you kissed me goodbye, let me go, and hoped that I'd come back. I'll always come back, Jay. Always."

With his arm around Dominic's waist, Jay gently moved them both to the couch. Blue pushed himself from Dominic's arms and snuggled down between them.

"I love you," he murmured. "I love you so much and I'm so thankful that you're as easy going as you are. Thank you."

"And thank you for loving me the way that you do."

Everything felt as though it was settling back down. Dominic curled himself onto the couch and rested his head against Jay's shoulder. Gently he stroked his fingers over the younger man's hair, his own eyes growing heavy as he watched the fire and listened to the rain.

~~~

Jay woke sated and aching in all of the right places. Dominic, demanding harlot that he could be, had made sure that they didn't fall asleep until the early hours of the morning. Stretching out in bed, Jay smile as he slowly woke.

"See that you've been playing the guitar." Dominic's voice was a whisper beside his ear and Jay rolled over to find his partner wrapped in a dressing grown and sitting on the edge of the bed. "I'm proud of you. Will you play for me one day?"

His smile widened as he took in Dominic's eager face. "One day, yeah. Maybe today."

Dominic's dark eyes lit up with hope. "Really?!"

Jay stretched a little more and felt his weary body settle into place. "Let's see how today goes. Just a thought – where were you when I texted you from the restaurant?"

A blush kissed Dominic's cheeks and the younger man looked sheepish with his dark hair falling into his eyes. "Just landed. I was getting ready to go to my car."

"Did you really fly home because you'd finished shopping?" Jay hoisted himself up into a sitting position and leaned back against the cool stone wall.

Dominic shrugged. "A little of that. A little because I missed you. A little because I wanted to come home. And a little because I wanted to prove that I wasn't cheating."

Those words broke Jay's heart and he reached out to pull the younger man into a hug. Before he could, Dominic swept up a folio of papers from the bedside table and presented them to Jay.

"Here. As promised. I want to hear you play it one day."

Taking the sheet music from Dominic, Jay read the faded words inscribed onto the red card cover. *Piano Concerto #2 – William S. Dalesworth*. It was a modern piece of music that had featured in dozens of adverts and a good handful of movies. Sweeping and evocative, it took Jay back to simpler, happier times. Times when he could be free without a care in the world. Tears began to mist his eyes and a lump crept up into his throat.

"I don't know what to say," he murmured.

An arm went around his shoulders and lips were pressed to his head. "Say nothing. Just play it for me one day."

"We don't have a piano."

"We don't," Dominic softly replied. "But the Stone Bridge Inn do. Sure they'll let you play it one night."

They sat like that for a littler longer before Blue interrupted them. The cat jumped up onto the bed and sat himself on Jay's knees. His amber eyes stared straight into his soul as he silently demanded to be fed.

"Okay. Okay." Jay sighed and untangled himself from Dominic. "Feeding time at the zoo."

With both Blue and Dominic hot on his heels, Jay made his way downstairs. Spring sun streamed through the windows and, as he was reaching for the cat food, Jay happened to glance at the back door.

"Oh no," he softly muttered.

Dominic stepped up behind him. "What?"

"Take a look at the door. I must be late feeding them."

Furry faces with expectant eyes and pricked ears stared at them through the glass panels of the doors.

"Deer!"

And before Jay could stop him, Dominic was hustling his way by to open the door.

"Dominic, don't let them in."

But it was too late. The back door had been flung open and Dominic had swept the cat up into his arms so that they could both look at the creatures in the garden.

Leaning against the counter with a pouch of cat

food in one hand, Jay watched as something strange happened. Ordinarily the deer kept their distance. They would take food from him but were quick to scamper back. With Dominic, they were pushing against one another to shove their faces into his free hand, nuzzling and bleating softly. Jay couldn't believe what he was seeing and he shook his head as he took in the blossoming relationship before him.

"Gotta feed 'em," Dominic finally said. "Did you say you have deer food?"

"I do. But how did you do that with them? They came right to you."

Even as Dominic turned to talk to him, two of the deer were inching their way into the cottage in a bid to follow their friend.

Dominic grinned at him. "They're my deer. The ones that have been coming to the store. They're gonna be pissed that I don't have pastries for them today."

Stunned, Jay just stared at him. Dominic's grin widened and he shrugged before trying to inch back passed Jay. Putting his arm out, he stopped the younger man in his tracks.

"I'm sorry, what?" he asked. "*Your* deer?!"

Dominic nodded.

"Dominic!" Jay sighed and shook his head before sinking back against the counter. "That's why they turned up here. You hadn't fed them for a few days and I suspect that they've been following your scent home. When you weren't at the shop they came here. I should be pissed at you."

From the corner of his eye he could see Dominic grinning. "But you're not because you've made new friends."

"They've given me something to do for the past few days, yes." He looked at Dominic and smirked. "Still gonna whoop your ass for it later."

Leaning closer, Dominic wrapped a hand in the back of his neck, his fingers tangling in the curls of Jay's silver hair, and gave him a long kiss. "If I remember rightly, that's a promise. But deer first. They're hungry. So is the cat, and so am I. And you could do with keeping your strength up if you wanna beat my ass later."

Jay looked at Dominic and then back at the deer in the kitchen. "Food's under the stairs. Feeder is up in the trees. Oatmeal for breakfast, okay?"

"Perfect!"

And with that, Dominic pulled away. He hauled the deer food out and was gone before Jay could draw another breath. Despite the ups and downs of the previous few days, life, it seemed, was returning to its normal, slightly chaotic, but thoroughly enjoyable, pace.

Printed in Great Britain
by Amazon

53025788R00078